Wild Ride
By: James Lyon

We all have people we like to dedicate our books to. This is my first time out, but I want to dedicate this novel to an ex of mine. She saw I had talent writing the kind of book you are about to read, and while the relationship never really went anywhere, and it's ten years later, I can't help but say without her, you wouldn't be reading this.

Wild Ride

Chapter 1

The sun lazily hit Andrew in the face as he tried to sleep in for a few minutes more. He had been working himself to the bone recently, and sometimes it felt like all he did was eat, work, shower, and sleep. He thought of the people he went to school with who complained about their partners and kids. Some part of him wished he had those problems. His main problem right now was that he had no time for a life despite having the money for it.

Getting out of bed, he felt like he was pushing sixty years old, not the thirty-odd years old that he was, and figured it must be a side effect of the post-work workout. He made his way to the kitchen on instinct and began his morning routine: getting the coffee started, feeding the cat, and grabbing a bowl of cereal. It was all done without him really thinking. He started reading the headlines and e-mails from the office on his tablet as he waited for the coffee to brew.

He browsed through his tablet; it seemed like things at work were under control, which meant one thing for him. It meant he was free to do as he pleased, and, best of all, it was summer! Which, in turn, meant he was free to indulge in one of his oldest vices—mountain biking! Not just riding a few kilometres, but going to the middle of nowhere and doing the off-road cycling that he loved.

With this information processed, he abandoned the cup of coffee in the maker as he took off around his apartment in a flash. Pajamas were stripped off as he changed into jean shorts and a black t-shirt; despite being an avid cyclist, he had never adapted to wearing spandex. Besides, it made him stand out if he chose to do normal activities during his travels. It was one thing to be a cyclist, it was another to stand out while doing so.

This was followed up by a quick once-over in the bathroom mirror to check on his appearance as he brushed his teeth. His brown hair was combed, his goatee a bit on the heavy side, but still trimmed. He deemed himself more than ready for a day of fun in the sun.

Next came loading up his backpack with some required equipment before checking the mechanics of his bike—he wasn't stupid enough to go cycling without even a casual check of his machine. Finding no large issues, he brought it down to his car. He knew he'd have to do some last-minute work on it when he got on site.

A quick walk around the car to ensure he didn't have a flat tire came back fine as well. He couldn't pass on a chance to look at himself in the driver's side mirror, even if he had to bend over a bit to accommodate his tall, six-foot-one frame. After that, he was off. He knew his cat could take care of himself for a day; he had made a point of leaving almost everything connected to the office behind him. He didn't want to be disturbed today as he had some fun. He knew he'd be back in a day's time, and life would continue as is. He'd be single, he'd have his work, his vices, but, in a sense, he'd be happy alone.

As his apartment building vanished from his car's rear-view mirror, little did he know life was about to change in a most unexpected way.

****

Erica woke up, and, half asleep as always, didn't even look at herself in her dresser mirror as she made her way to the kitchen to get her morning coffee started. Trying to keep herself upright, she managed to stumble into the shower. Even before the first jets of water hit her, her hands knew precisely which gauge went where so the water was not too hot or too cold. As the water began to rain down on her, she started to grab various beauty products by memory as she washed her black hair and her body down. Wouldn't have done her any good to show up as work a mess, especially given how she owned the business.

As the smell of fresh coffee started to waft into the shower, she turned it off, grabbing a white towel off a rack along the wall to dry herself off with. She knew housekeeper would come by later to replace it as she cleaned the house up. Semi-awake, Erica was able to admire herself in a mirror that hung off the wall in the hallway. Despite being over thirty years old, her large breasts were as perky as they were when she was a teen. She knew if she had been human, they'd have gotten her tons of male attention due to how large they were. Her purple eyes—with epicanthic folds—matched the purple dye job she'd recently had done to the ends of her black hair. More than a few of her suppliers had complimented her on her look after she'd had it done.

Walking into the kitchen, she raised the towel onto her shoulders as she started to finish making herself a coffee. Grabbing some fruit and some breakfast muffins that were heavy on oats, she was finally starting to feel ready for the day. Finishing it all off, she made her way back to her bedroom to get dressed.

It didn't take too long—a bra here, a white blouse there—and, with a sense of ceremony, she put on a gold chain necklace with a heart-shaped locket to complete the look. Looking at her reflection in the mirror with her blunt, bobbed haircut, she deemed herself presentable. It also made her think of how Mom had texted her, once again reminding her it was long since past time to find a husband, and make some babies. It wasn't her fault her last boyfriend hadn't measured up when it had mattered most, and she remembered a few times before that she had failed when put to the same test.

She did her best to brush out the light, brown hair that covered the lower half of her body, including her four legs. More than a few employees had complained about the horse smell in the office. What did they think they were getting into when they applied to work at a place called the Centaur Café? That they'd be working for a fairy that smelled of bubble gum and roses?

It was the whole reason she had started to shower in the morning in the first place, as a concession to her employees who had threaten to quit if she didn't do something about that horse smell that penetrated the office at times.

As much as she wanted to linger around her house, she knew she had to be at the office as soon as it opened up. Grabbing a light blue jacket along with saddle bags as she made her way out the front door of her one-story house, she couldn't help but think about things a bit. She knew that, despite what her mother said, she'd find a man when a man came into her life that was worthy of her and vice versa. Until then, all she could do was try her best to enjoy her life, one day at a time.

With that, she started off on a leisurely ten-kilometre run through the woods before hitting the city and being forced to walk the rest of the way to work.

****

It had taken Andrew almost until noon to leave the modern world behind him, and find the deepest entrance to Queens Dale Woods for his satisfaction. It was a natural park about three hundred kilometres north of Ottawa, Ontario, Canada. Out here, barely any cell phones worked; in fact, every five or ten kilometres on the highway up here, there was a sign saying "phone," pointing in a direction for motorists who had car problems. Andrew had never had to use them, but half suspected those phones were free, given how they were there for emergencies.

He turned into the park the ranger was kind enough to give him directions to—one of the deeper parking lots available to the public. Paying his fee, he could hear the gravel road beneath his car as he kept driving. He had turned off the radio a while back to just enjoy the silence. Most people when they go off-roading complain about the other people there, but it was not a problem for Andrew. A lot of millennials were afraid of going anywhere without a coffee shop, cell service, or where their parents couldn't get them out of trouble in a flash. Those things were precisely what he wanted to get away from.

Finding a parking spot was easy for two reasons—it was deep in the park, and it was a weekday. Unpacking the bike, he did some last-minute tune-up work on it, before proclaiming it ready. Leaning it up against the side of the car, he pulled out his beaten-up backpack from the back of it, along with his cycling shoes, those shoes being his sole concession to looking the part of a cyclist. Tightening the shoes, he looked back to the passenger's side seat of his car where his cell phone lay. He knew it was useless, but sometimes there were strange instances where cells did work where they weren't supposed to. After mulling it over for a few moments, he left it behind; if he really wanted to take some photos, he always had a digital camera in his backpack that did a far superior job than any cell camera ever did.

Mounting his bike, he rode off into the entrance of the woods. He couldn't help but admire the greenery around him—every tree was an evergreen that seemed to reach to the sky and beyond. Except for the trail leading into the forest, there was barely a sign of man's hand here. Naturally there was a map to the side of the entrance, and he barely gave it half a glance. He had been at this sport for years, and knew how to follow the official and unofficial trails, as well as find his way back to where he started without a map of any kind. Sometimes one of the joys and sorrows in life was finding out it was harder all the time to find new land to explore. If Alexander could weep at no new lands to conquer, then, as a rider, Andrew could weep there were fewer new lands to explore, that he had to travel this far to find them.

Taking it all in, he took off into the woods, not knowing what to expect, and at times like this, Andrew loved the unexpected when he didn't know or care what was beyond the next tree or mountain.

****

If Andrew was loving the unexpected, Erica was hating it. Here she was, the owner of a multi-city café chain, reduced to working the cash. The reason she was working as a cashier was because a café on the south side of Yanapeachu city was already short on people, and an Elf had been quite upset over a comment made by a Minotaur this morning regarding her ears. This led to the only person from the head office who could be spared for a few hours being sent out here to help out, meaning Erica.

Given how Erica had founded the company ten years ago, back when it was just her, there was something very symbolic about having to resume the role of cashier, even for a short while. It also meant putting on the uniform, which consisted of a French maid's bonnet and apron. She was still able to wear her white blouse she had been wearing earlier.

It was, in fact, situations like this that had led to her designing the Centaur Cafés the way she did—where the cashier was in a booth where she or he took the order, but for the most part, the back of the café was blocked off from the viewing public. This was because despite Yanapeachu being a non-human city, there was still plenty of racism to go around. More than once, police had been called into various businesses because an Elf didn't like the fact a Dwarf worked there, or a Gnome had a problem with a Harpy doing electrical work.

The setup made it so the customer only saw the cashier from the waist up, and if you used the drive-through, you saw no one. This tended to keep the random complaints of racism down. She had learned that lesson three months after opening the first location when a Swan Maiden had accused a Harpy of trying to kill her because of some ancient bad blood between their people.

Rubbing one of her temples at the memory of that little lawsuit, it was part of the standard employee agreement now. If you had any racial reasons to hate another race, you left it at the door if you wanted to work for Centaur Café. Failure to honour that part of the labor agreement led to the withdrawal of said employment offer. Professional complaints, as always, were heard, and accommodations made when possible.

Looking at the clock, she saw it was a little past two p.m.—three more hours to go and they'd close up for the day, and, with any luck, personnel would find someone to replace her by morning. Still, she had done a good job; she had kept the lunch line moving, and she could hear people in the back cleaning up. That's when she heard someone walking in, which snapped her attention to the door.

She was immediately shocked that a human of all things had even reached Yanapeachu City, given how both the Human and Non-Human governments had taken big strides to ensure both populations never met. This had been in place for centuries, since the peak of a global war where one man had died to separate the two peoples. Technically, this human wasn't here illegally, but to get here, either he took a rare road that connected the two civilizations, or he had passed several "do not pass" signs if he had come from the woods.

Looking him over, she came to the conclusion that he had come here from the woods, given how everything he wore was covered in a layer of dirt, and strangely enough, he was smiling. As he walked up to her, she could hear a clicking sound from his shoes she had never heard before in her life, with each step he took. The sound reminded her a bit of her own hooves when she walked on tiles.

As he approached the main cash, he seemed oblivious to the glares he was receiving from the other guests, who, until now, had been involved in their own things. With each step he took, the helmet that hung off the side of his backpack swayed until he was face to face with her. "Excuse me. I'd like to order some food please?"

Putting her hands together, she replied in her British accent, hoping he understood her, "Certainly, sir, what would you like to eat today?"

Looking over the menu board, he began to list the ingredients he wanted for a submarine sandwich, and Erica began to dutiful enter it into the computer when the screen died. She made a comment about the faulty computer, and she was about to pick up the phone to call tech support when he asked, "May I?" as he looked at the faulty computer.

"Sir, you can't come around to the other side of the cash, so I don't see how you can fix the computer. Just please let me call tech support."

Raising an eyebrow, he asked, "What harm can I do?" Looking at her name badge, he continued, "Erica, is it?"

Realizing he'd help either way, she replied, "No harm at all."

Erica had been sensing him since he'd arrived, nothing intrusive, only his Qi, his life force. It let her get to know him at a level that went beyond his physical appearance. It was something she did with everyone she met, and it had helped her out on countless occasions during social interactions. As he bent down to work on the computer, their hands briefly touched and it was like raw energy passed from him to her. She had only felt this way a few times in her life, and she knew what she wanted to do next. Andrew couldn't see it, but behind the cash, one of her rear legs had bent up on instinct. As he continued to examine the computer, questions began to bubble in the back of her mind, but before she could voice any of them, he said, "Here is your problem."

She watched as he tightened a connection from the cash to the screen, which promptly lit up. "Looks like the connection to your VGA port got loose, it happens with time. You might want to replace the cable when you get a chance."

"Thank you," she replied. "I'm sorry, I didn't get your name."

"Andrew," he said as way of introduction, extending his hand. She shook it, and once again she felt that raw surge of energy. He didn't try to squeeze her hand, but grasped it firmly. Clearly he wasn't like some men who thought it was a good idea to use a gesture of peace to prove a point.

Smiling and blushing slightly, she was glad that the way she'd styled her hair hid her eyes and cheeks a bit. "I am wondering, Andrew, would you mind sharing a bite to eat with me?" she asked coyly.

"Erica," he said in protest, "I wouldn't want to get you in any trouble with your boss for skipping work."

"Oh, I am sure the boss wouldn't mind."

As he reached into his wallet to pay for the sub, she promptly stopped him. "This is on the house. Think of it as a way of management expressing its gratitude for fixing the computer."

"All right," he said. Looking towards the free table on the terrace, he asked, "Meet you there once my sub is ready?"

"Certainly."

Once the cash window was closed, she was in motion, apron and bonnet on the hooks beside the window. After a few quick text messages to the office, she ran into the kitchen and saw the sub being made, as well as some soup she had asked for. Grabbing the food before the conveyer belt could bring it outside, she walked over to where the dishes were being washed. As was expected, Ruby was up to her shoulders as she washed the dishes. This wasn't because Ruby loved the water, it was because at three-foot-six tall, she didn't have very long arms. Addressing the pink-haired gnome from behind, Erica said, "Ruby, could I have your attention for a moment, please?"

Hopping off her stool, Ruby ran over to Erica, and tilted her head up so she could look her boss in the eye. "SurebosswhatcanIdoforyou?"

One of the dangers of talking with Ruby was that she spoke so fast, everything appeared to become one giant word. Strangely enough, if you believed her resumé, she was over fifty years old, and held two PHDs. Which meant she was extremely over qualified to work as a dishwasher, but she seemed happy doing it.

Speaking slowly, Erica said, "I need you to cover the cash for me until the end of the day, and I know you've wanted to work on it for a while."

Smiling like she'd just found out all of her favourite holidays had been combined into one, Ruby said in her high-pitched voice, "Youmeanit?"

"Yes, and if you do a good job, I'll tell your manager you can work the cash from now on as a reward. However, good means no talking the customers' ears off, and speaking slowly."

"Yeah, thankyouErica, thankyou, thankyou, thankyou," the little gnome said before taking off in a burst of speed, as was her way, to get dressed for the role of cashier. Erica figured offhand that it was a win-win. If Ruby did a good job, then they could hire a Slime person to wash the dishes, and if she did a bad job, the company had a good reason not to employ her in that capacity.

Before stepping outside with the food, Erica stepped into the employee's bathroom to look herself over in the mirror. Grabbing a makeup kit from one of her saddle bags, she reapplied a bit of it here and there. Looking at her blouse, she undid the first few buttons to expose some cleavage; she had heard human males loved large-breasted women. She knew she was nervous, and she hadn't been like this in ages. It was just a man, a meal, and, looking down at her heart-shaped locket, maybe something more. It had been such a long time since she'd felt strongly about anyone; even when she'd met her last boyfriend, it had felt iffy. However, before she would do anything, she had to get to know Andrew first. She was a woman, not an animal (even if half of her was).

Leaving the bathroom, she walked out into the café and saw him sitting on the terrace. Balancing the tray with ease, she thought that there was no time like the present to get to know him.

****

Andrew was sitting back, trying to relax and enjoy the summer heat. He had done several hours worth of cycling and he felt it. His legs were aching for either an icepack or something else cold. He just wished he had been smart enough to order a cold drink when he ordered his meal. Given his time with the sport, he had been smart enough to freeze a few water bottles and pack them with him. Pulling one out and rubbing it over his thighs, he closed his eyes and let out a sigh of contentment. He couldn't help it, given how good it felt.

As he had reflected in the past, there were days, there were bad days, there were his bad days. With the wind gently flowing though his brown hair, he couldn't help but think the opposite was true. There were days, there were good days, there were his good days. Despite being a semi-confirmed bachelor, he couldn't help but have a fantasy or two about the cute cashier who had made a play on him at the café. He had learned the hard way years ago that his vices and those of women tended to be too different for a real relationship sadly.

He had been so lost in thought, he'd missed Erica's approach until the last moment. In retrospect, he'd assumed it had been a horse approaching. It wasn't until she semi-cleared her throat and said, "Andrew?"

Getting up from the chair, he apologized. Looking her over, he could see she had applied some deep red lipstick and blush, and then he saw the problem. "I'd like to offer you a seat, but your"—he paused for a moment, looking for the right word—"costume? Seems to make it hard to take one." He looked at the horse half where her tail was swishing back and forth. "Maybe you'd feel better if you got out of it?"

Erica couldn't help but laugh a bit as she passed the tray to Andrew. "Trust me, it's a little hard for me to get out of it," she said as she raised her rear end in what she hoped was a convincing display that she had human legs and feet in her horse half.

Andrew cleared away a chair, giving Erica the space she required to lower herself down, "Must be hard to use the washroom in that get-up," he said as he sat down himself, grabbing the first six inches of his foot-long sub.

Smiling coyly, she responded, "Oh, you live and work with something long enough, you adapt. In fact the whole city is preparing for a big cosplay convention so everyone is dressing up." She started to dig into her soup. "So, what brings you to Yanapeachu? Work? Pleasure? Family?"

"Pleasure," he responded firmly. He then explained his journey through the woods, and how, after several different turns on unofficial trails, he had found his way here. "I've never heard of Yanapeachu before." Looking around the city with all its different people, none of them looking remotely human, he said, "I spend a lot of time on the road, I am surprised to find a city this big so far north, just like it seems weird to see everyone dressing for cosplay."

Glancing away from Erica for a moment, he looked at the people moving around them. He added, "I've never heard of people cosplaying to this level of detail and walking around in public." Some part of Andrew's mind was having a hard time accepting all this.

"You know how it is," she replied. "The farther north you go, the harder it is to get people to want to move there, so local businesses made a mass appeal to the geeks and nerds. They were told they could cosplay at work if they moved up here." Looking down for a moment, Erica doubted Andrew would know she was ashamed of the fact she was lying to him. She didn't like lying, but she also knew the rule of her people. Humans couldn't know the truth unless they married into or had a direct connection with the community, the only exception to this rule being government officials.

"Shame I missed that call when it happened, I might've taken some employers up on it." Looking around, he saw several "Help Wanted" signs. "Then again, maybe I can, shame I left my phone in my car. Hard to hand out even digital resumés without it."

"Maybe you can do it later, since the future is always full of possibilities."

"Sounds like something from a fortune cookie."

"Hey, just because I dress up like a Centaur, doesn't mean I totally ignore my Asian heritage," she said indignantly, and, as if to emphasize her point, she crossed her arms underneath her breasts.

Despite barely knowing her, he knew she was playing with him. "Still, all things considered, this might be my kind of town." Looking around, he said, "Fine women," raising part of his sub to Erica as a salute. "I saw a few stores that have stuff I want to buy, before I found your café."

"Sounds like Yanapeachu was made for you," she replied, hastily adding, "If you were looking to move somewhere. Do you have deep roots where you live?"

"Nope, most of my work and friends are on the net. My boss tells me where to go, I go, get the job done, rinse, repeat. How about you?"

"Most of my friends live in the city, or nearby it."

"That include a boyfriend?"

"No. We broke up a few months ago. Things weren't working out."

"Ouch, what happened?"

"You know how it is, some guys just can't measure up to family expectations."

"Did your family make the decision for you to dump him, or you?"

"I did ultimately," she said sternly.

"How about we change subjects? Since I get this sense that relationships are a bit of a sore point for you. And there is something I'm wondering about you..."

Erica signalled for one of her waiters to bring her a soda, and Andrew nodded that he'd like one also. "Well then, shoot, I tend to be an open book," she prompted.

Looking at her locket, Andrew tried to ignore her breasts, despite their size and his attraction to them. "That locket you wear, does it mean something? I mean, it seems a bit big for a picture or two."

Looking down at it, she replied, "It does, but it's personal. Maybe we can talk about it later?"

"All right."

"Hey, you mentioned earlier that you saw a few stores that sell stuff you want to buy, what are they?"

"You seriously want to know?"

"Wouldn't ask if I didn't want to."

"Used books, vintage video games. With everyone going eBook these days, it's harder and harder to find physical bookstores, much less the used ones. I love looking for holes in the wall that sell that kind of stuff."

"I know what you mean about places like those being hard to find. It was one of the reasons I moved to Yanapeachu several years ago."

So it began; they started to talk like they had known each other all their lives. They talked about video games they had played, books they had read. Occasional one of them would mention something the other didn't know about, and it began a gentle give and take. Andrew was keeping a mental tally of how many people were cosplaying, even if they were practising, and wondering if there was more going on than it seemed. It wasn't until it was a bit past five that Ruby came up to them, keeping a respectful distance, and whispered, "Excuse me."

They ignored her, given how they were locked in conversation, so Ruby then shouted in her high-pitched voice, "Excuse me!"

Shocked out of her conversation about some of the local trails, Erica responded to Ruby. "Yes?"

Trying to be as polite as possible, the gnome said, addressing them both, "It is five o'clock, and the café is due to close for the day. The staff would like to go home, my lady and sir."

Looking down at Ruby, Erica, practically begging with her eyes, said, "Could you give us like fifteen more minutes, please?"

Despite Ruby's normally bubbly personality, there seemed to be something firm in her voice as she said, "I think we can swing that, but the boss won't be happy paying overtime."

Smiling through gritted teeth, Erica responded, "I am sure the boss won't mind in this instance."

"Very well," said the gnome smugly as she walked back into the café.

"Where were we?" Erica asked as she focused on Andrew.

He stopped her for a moment. "Before we pick up where we left off, shouldn't you be concerned that the boss won't authorize overtime for your coworkers?"

Leaning back as far as she could, drinking some water she had ordered as they had been talking, she reassured him. "Trust me, the boss won't have a problem authorizing a bit of overtime."

"You sure? I had a boss years ago who had a fit because I logged fifteen minutes of it without his consent."

"Andrew, don't worry about it, I know the boss very well." In fact, she thought, even if the manager got mad, she wouldn't say one word since the final boss said yes.

"Mind if I ask you an odd question?"

"Shoot," she said.

"Why do you dress up as a Centaur? I mean, there has to be easier things to dress up as."

Erica's first response was to say she was born one, but she instead replied, "You could say it was a race I felt I was born to cosplay."

"That still doesn't explain it," replied Andrew, his face filled with confusion. "I've seen shows where they show the work involved in making people look like you do, and it's not easy, or fast."

"Maybe I like the statement it makes about me?"

"Statement about you? I am sorry, I know the different races in fantasy, but not everything about them."

"Centaurs were seen as both warriors and teachers by the ancient Greeks," Erica said, "and I find it something worth trying to be, and it shows how no people are as one-dimensional as they appear to be."

"It can't be easy getting in and out of that costume when your day is over, much less going to the bathroom, and you need a lot of room to move around in it."

"True, but it does make me happy, and reminds me of who I am," Erica said, keeping her voice light and chuckling a little at her own comment. *If only he knew the truth,* she thought. Continuing with a more serious voice, she said, "Day to day, it's hard, but when I get a chance to cut loose, it's worth it. Humans can run fast, but nothing compares to the speed a horse body gives you." As she said this, she ran a hand over her horse half.

Smiling like a kindred spirit, Andrew said, "I know what you mean about that need for speed. To hear that hidden music within all of us. I never had the idea of designing a horse body to see if it'd go faster than a mountain bike."

"But surely as a—" She had to stop herself for a moment before she gave herself away, and then continued, "as a man of means, who owns a car, you can go faster in that car any day."

"Cars are fine, but even when you cut loose in them, you feel like a passenger, like it's going on around you, but you're not connected to the speed you're a part of."

"Hmm, I'll take your word for it."

"You don't drive?"

"No, my lifestyle doesn't really need a car." With a mischievous tone in her voice, she asked, "Hey, I'm wondering... Are you up for a race? Mountain bike versus my horse body?" She knew her tone of voice was a lie—inside, she was shaking like a leaf. Few people outside her race knew what she was asking of him; as a human, he had no chance of knowing the stakes of the race she was proposing.

"Erica, are you sure that's a good idea? I mean, I just met you, and I don't want to risk damaging what looks like a valuable costume just to see what is fast."

"Andrew, I live in this costume almost all day long, I know what it can do," she said, getting ready to stand her ground. As far as she was concerned, there was no way they were going to leave here and not race.

"You are certain it won't be damaged?"

"Nothing a little time won't fix, if you do cause me to break it while we race."

"All right, Erica," he said confidently. "I just don't want

you to be mad at me if you break something that appears to be very valuable to you by racing me when you barely know me."

This race will tell me everything I need to know about you and more, Andrew, she thought. "Trust me, I have a good warranty plan covering it."

Behind his dark sunglasses, she saw a familiar glimmer of competition in his eyes, as he responded by saying, "I assume you'd want to do it right now. So where is the finish line, and would there be a prize?"

Pointing to a solitary hill in the distance where a giant tree seemed to dominate the sky, she said, "How about the top of that hill? We'll figure out the prize when we're done the race. Cool?"

Looking over the mountain, Andrew could already see several trails weaving their way through the trees, even at this distance. "You mean the one facing west, where the sun is setting on it?"

"Yes, that's the one."

A smile touched his lips as he said, "Game on! Any rules you want to set for our race?"

"How about we keep pace until we hit the bottom of the hill, which will be the starting line. That way neither of us can cheat when we really do race to the top."

"Makes sense. I don't know the way."

"And once we hit the bottom, we split up and are committed to any path we take."

"Done," he said. If she was reading him right, he was going to relish this race like her. Getting up herself, she couldn't help but admire his legs and butt. True, he wasn't a Centaur like her, but she couldn't help but apply their sense of sexual taste to him. While, like all races, Centaurs admired fit beings, there was a special weakness for legs and butts with them. Strong legs and butts meant good runners, and the horse part of them loved that. As Andrew bent down to unlock his bike, she wished he was wearing spandex, but tight jean shorts were just as fine.

Forcing herself to stay focused, she reminded herself that no matter how attractive a being was, tradition had to be observed, especially with humans. One of her hands strayed to her saddle bag, where she pressed several buttons on a tablet held within it. Turning around so she could focus on the mountain, she held up her heart-shaped locket. *Let the bones of fate be rolled, and let us handle the results*, she thought.

Chapter 2

It hadn't taken much doing to get some improvised help to set up the start of the race. Traffic was light, so it was easy for Andrew and Erica to line up on the other side of the street. Ruby had dragged a tall chair from the café across the street so she was a little higher than both racers. The staff of the café had gathered outside to watch it start.

One could almost feel the tension in the air as both competitors waited for Ruby to give the go, even if her start flag was a dishwashing towel. At almost a moment's notice, she dropped the flag shouting, "Go, go, go, go, go!"

With that, both Andrew and Erica took off in an instant, even if the first part of the race was the pacing part so Erica could guide Andrew to the mountain. Waiting until they were clearly out of sight, Ruby picked the chair up over her head, walked calmly across the street, and put the chair down while her coworkers broke out their cellphones with calls to different Centaur Cafés and head office. Getting on top of the chair, Ruby began to take bets on the outcome of the race. She had been watching Erica and Andrew all afternoon, and while she didn't know everything, she could suspect. Given how one of her PHDs was in probability, she was looking to clean up.

****

How long had it been since she let herself go like this, thought Erica. Where even if they were pacing, they were racing. She could see it in his eyes; if she sped up, he matched her, and then she saw a side of him she knew she could love right from the start. Sometimes, for no explicable reason, he'd make his bike jump—not over the moon, but enough to get some air time with it. It was childish on a certain level, but it showed his exuberance for life. Maybe that is why she wasn't attracted to Centaurian men; none of the ones she had dated had any sense of fun. Other species do, and while there were exceptions to every rule, it was like sifting for gold from sand—ninety-nine percent of the time, you only found sand.

In many ways, Andrew's own thoughts mirrored that of Erica. How long had it been since he had really raced, he wondered. While he had never gone professional or even semi, when he went cycling he was always on the lookout for another cyclist to see who could go faster. He knew from first-hand experience how the breakdown went. On roads like this, the speed bikes would dominate him, on off-roads, he'd dominate them, and street bikes could go to either place, but they lost in both. He couldn't help but wonder how this race would turn out; he had never raced someone cosplaying, much less cosplaying as a Centaur.

Regardless, in a sense they were the same. As they raced out of town towards the hill, he could see it in her eyes when he spared her a glance. The same look that filled his eyes, filled hers as they navigated past people, traffic, and all manner of obstacles. It was cold, calculating, but it was as tightly connected to their need for speed as their very souls. They could no more lose that part of themselves willingly than they could separate a limb from their bodies.

As road gave way to gravel trails, Erica stopped for a moment right after they had passed under a wooden archway. Reaching around her neck, she went to remove her locket. It was only then that Andrew realized how massive it was, given how she could barely hold it in one of her hands. Stopping beside her, he said, "I figured out what I want as my prize when this race is over, and I win."

"Oh?"

"I'd like to know what is in that locket, and why you carry it."

Smiling as mysteriously as the Mona Lisa while putting the locket in a saddle bag, she replied, "Well, let's see who wins first."

Looking up the mountain, Andrew could feel the adrenaline rushing though his veins—the cycle here was just a warm up. Extending a hand to Erica, he said, "Good luck."

"Likewise."

Shaking hands as equals, per the rules of the contest, they went their separate ways. What none of them saw was a gate rising to block off all retreat. They were committed until they both reached the
top of the mountain.

****

As Erica pushed herself into a full run, she was so embarrassed of her body. Andrew hadn't seen it, or smelled it, but she was soaking wet. Even during that short pacing with him, her horse side had wanted him, and the worst part was, short of becoming angry at him, she had no real way to control that side of herself. As she started to climb the mountain, she wondered if human women had this problem, where instinct overrode intellect when it came time to select a mate.

The reason why her people had developed the race as a way to test potential mates was to honour the ways of their violent past, where only the best and most fierce Centaurs earned the right to breed. It had led to more than a few battles to the death where, strangely enough, the winner would've accepted the loser as a mate, but the loser died in the battle.

Normally the idea of running the Marriage Race after such a brief meeting wouldn't even be considered. Centaurs were a race of tradition, and tradition did not say you try to get married after knowing someone for less than twelve hours. However, the laws regarding humans were simple and clear. Humans could not interact with Non-Humans, unless they were government officials, or had a connection by marriage into Non-Human society. Despite the laws, the history, and traditions in play, her heart told her she had made the right call.

She just hoped that if Andrew won, that he would forgive her deceptions and accept her as his bride. Not that she was going to go down without a fight. This wasn't the first time she had felt this way about a mate, and she wasn't one to surrender no matter how she felt. Seeing a split ahead of her, she chose the path to the right. If Andrew was to become a member of the Non-Humans, he'd have to prove himself like everyone else. If he was to accept her in defeat, she didn't want anyone who was watching the replays thinking she hadn't given it her all.

****

There were days, there were good days, and there were great days as far as Andrew was concerned. All right, he hadn't had a chance to go shopping in Yanapeachu beyond visiting a café. However, there were other ways to mark it down as a win.

Finding a whole town of people who shared his interests was a major win. He hoped, when this was all over, he could return here with his car. Maybe make some time to visit Erica when they both weren't working. With her lean, Asian face, he suspected her ancestry was most likely Chinese, or Japanese. He had felt embarrassed that several times during their conversation, he had caught himself staring at her large breasts.

This was the twenty-first century, and men were supposed to be gentlemen. It all depended on the woman, and with the #MeToo movement, it was hard to know where the line was sometimes. Yes, he had seen she had put some makeup on for what was a casual meal. He didn't know if she had exposed herself to attract him, or to dare him to do something to get himself in trouble.

It had been a while since he had felt such attraction to a woman, and he knew on some level it was mutual. It was an ancient dance they were involved in, male and female attracted to one another, with a child and the future blazing on ahead. Shaking his head to keep his mind on the race, he could feel the sweat rolling off his back as it hit his backpack. All this thinking of love and attraction would do him a fat lot of good if he lost this race. He suspected more was on the line than Erica had let on.

Coming up the hill, he could feel his legs burning—his bike was designed for going downhills, not up them! Upon cresting the hill, he saw a rickety, old bridge that looked like it'd fall apart at a moment's notice. The water below it didn't look too inviting either, given how it was rushing off a small waterfall not far from him. To someone on foot, it might be almost inviting, but to a cyclist, nope, nada, too deep. He thought it was time to change the rules, or rather, his shoes. Over the years, nature had dug a small channel in the earth and soil. While his cycling shoes couldn't climb it, he was confident that he could in his normal shoes.

Stopping for a moment, he went about changing them. He didn't know if this broke the rules, but given how he wasn't turning back, and he saw a trail above him, he hoped this fell within the accepted ones.

****

Erica knew she had lost the second the tablet had gone off. Andrew had crossed the finish line. The sun was setting, and several times as she rounded a part of the hill, she had seen smoke from the fire on top of it. She was beat, her body was soaked with sweat, and now it was just a matter of making it to the top with some sense of dignity. Weak from lack of water, she cursed herself a fool—why didn't she think to bring provisions when she undertook this race? She knew her horse half metabolism demanded more than her human half, especially when she raced with it.

"Erica!" She could hear Andrew running towards her. Grabbing her underneath her breasts to help steady her and support her weight, he said, "I am sorry, I don't mean anything sexual by this." Erica leaned on him while he continued, saying, "We've got to get you out of this costume! You look like hell on earth." She could hear the concern in his voice.

In a very real sense, his words were dead on. During the race, her makeup had started to run, she had ripped the sleeves off her white blouse to let the cooling air energize her. The brief energy boost hadn't helped her win.

Smiling, she replied under her breath, "All I did was race."

From his backpack, he pulled out a water bottle to give to her that she downed as they crossed the wooden archway on top of the hill. By crossing under it together, she knew all the hidden cameras would be turned off, and, in a sense, by being willing to sacrifice his clear victory, Andrew had just risen his stock among the Centaurs', even if he chose to return to the human world.

Andrew passed her another water bottle, and, like the first one, it helped refresh her. She told him to take a seat on the log and she stood across from him on the other side of the fire. It was so late into the night that it was well past sunset. Now came the moment of truth, she thought. Looking him straight in the eyes, she lowered herself as best she could with her front hooves in a bow, saying, "Congratulations on your victory, my lord."

"Erica, I am no lord. Now please let me help you get out of that costume," Andrew said as he got up. He started to look her over, frantically trying to find a seam to help her out of it.

Struggling to get up, she replied, "Yes, my 'costume.'" She made quotation marks with her hands as she said the word costume. "It's tied to the locket, and several other things, but more importantly, the one thing you earned that I won't deny you tonight. The truth."

"The truth?"

Despite how weak she felt, she got up, her legs shaking. She took a few steps back away from the fire so Andrew could see the lights from Yanapeachu in the distance. "Yanapeachu and other cities like it are inhabited by Non-Human Sentient Beings," she explained. "Over one thousand years ago, due to countless conflicts with humans, our people signed a treaty enforced to this day. It stated simply that we are to avoid all possible contact with humans."

The implications of her statement hit Andrew like a ton of bricks. He was a normal man, not some secret agent, and it seemed he just cycled deep into this whole new possible life. Stepping back to face her, Andrew said, "So you really are a Centaur? And by people, you mean more than one race? Does that explain all the different coplayers I saw in the city?"

"Yes, to everything."

Looking her in the eye, he asked, "May I?"

"May I?" She seemed confused before realizing suddenly what he meant. "Oh, certainly," she said as she lifted part of her blouse up.

Getting up close, Andrew ran his hand along the line where human flesh gave way to horse flesh in disbelief as he said in a hushed tone, "Incredible."

Erica let of a quick laugh and said in protest, "Be careful, I am ticklish there."

"Sorry."

Despite her state of mind, Erica said in a playful tone, "Been like this my whole life." Andrew looked her over, but not in a sexual sense. It was like when he saw her, he wasn't seeing her in a sexual way, or a monster, but as a normal person of all things. This is amazing, she thought. She knew his warrior spirit wouldn't let him finish second in the race, but him accepting her as much as he'd accept another human was surprising.

As he stopped checking her out, Erica lowered her blouse. With their proximity, she could feel her loins warming again. Gods above and below, she wanted this man; he had beaten her honourably in a race. It was now a matter of him accepting all this.

Andrew asked her, "You called me 'my lord' before. How does that fit into all this? And why do I smell something very sugary nearby?" The last comment caused him to look around, confused and sniffing the air.

Looking down towards her chest, she said, "I called you My Lord because..."

"Because?"

As quietly as she could, she continued, and Andrew strained his ears to hear her. "Because you just won what my people, by tradition, call the Marriage Race. If you will accept this defeated one, I will become your wife tonight, from now and until we both pass on to the next life."

Andrew took a few steps back. "So there is no hidden camera crew nearby to film this?"

"None, we have different ways of verifying it."

Then, to Erica's surprise, Andrew became suspicious of all things; she could see it in his body and hear it in his voice as he said, "How about some other way to let me make a fool of myself, and to record it for posterity?"

Sounding as sincere as possible, Erica said, "Andrew, what's wrong with you?"

Getting up, Andrew walked away from her. Shifting his head towards the city, Erica could only see half his face in the campfire as he said, "Erica, this just seems too good to be true. Horse half or no horse half, I find you attractive."

"Then what's wrong? When we spoke earlier, you said you had no one special in your life."

"My ex and I did part ways on bad terms and it was years ago, and I guess my heart wants to accept this, but my mind doesn't." With that, he seemed lost in thought, not saying a word.

Getting up, despite how tired she was, she walked up beside up, and put an arm around his shoulders, "Andrew, I am not her."

"I know."

"Then why do you seem so on guard?"

Still not turning to her, he said, "Look at me, Erica. I am a loser. I am over thirty, single—heck, most people have had countless sexual partners by my age, and I can count the number of women I've been with on one hand."

Erica could feel it from him as he finished the sentence. He didn't think he was a loser, he was just saying that since that is what human society had told him. He was angry with the hand he had been dealt, but something told her he was also selective about his partners. It wasn't ego, it wasn't pride, it was in his core to be selective of who he slept with. It was a part of him always looking for someone, and finding many people wanting. "Is that what you think I am?" she asked him. She wanted to kiss him, to let him know she accepted him as he was, because so far, every indication was he was willing to accept her as she was. She also knew the odds of finding a man as close to pure as she was were astronomical.

"How does my sex life connect to you being a loser?"

"You know I've had my share of rejections over the years."

"Something tells me there is more to this than you are telling me."

"There is." She so wanted to look him in the eye, and tell him about the men her mother had introduced her to over the years, rejecting them after a simple scan of who they were.

"Where does that leave us?"

"I guess the question is, do you want to accept your victory and get married to me?" Speeding up a bit, she rambled, "I know this is a lot to take in, and I am sorry if I wasn't honest with you from the start."

She saw just a hint of a smile touch his lips as he said, "How do we complete this ritual of yours?"

Giving a suggestive shake of her hindquarters along with a wink, she said, "I think you can figure out how."

Turning around in unison, they both faced the fire as they kept talking. Andrew relaxed a bit and put an arm around her, drawing her closer to him.

"Are we—?"

"Yes, if we...mated, I could carry children made by us."

"Could or will?"

"I am on the pill, so not this time."

"Would anything—?"

"Nothing strange would happen to you, if we mated. STDs tend to not be able to jump species, and I am clean as far as I know, if that is your concern."

He asked her, "I take it this is one of the ways a human can know about your people?"

"Yes. Understand, Andrew, if it weren't for the treaty, I'd wait longer before initializing the ritual, despite how attracted I am to you physically, and to your Qi."

"If it makes you feel any better, Erica, I had planned to ask you out after the race, despite the fact that I've been a happy bachelor for a while," he said, smiling. It had felt like a lifetime since he had had the nerve to ask someone out. Erica saw just a hint of a blush cross his face even in the dim firelight.

Good, she thought, the attraction was mutual. Andrew walked over to the log, and, with a hand gesture, invited her to sit down and join him. After she did, he wrapped an arm around her and asked, "Am I bound by this treaty? Will I be forbidden to return to the human world if we...mated tonight?"

Leaning into him, she said, "No, and in time, if your close friends and family wanted to come here, arrangements could be made. I mean, we do trade with the human world sometimes, after all." Trade seemed like such a secondary issue right now with her heart on the line, and the way he said "mated" made it sound so clinical. Like insert tab A into slot B, baby C pops out a while later.

She could see him lost in thought, just keeping a protective arm around her, until he broke the silence by saying, "There is more to this, isn't there?"

"Yes."

Gears still turning in his mind, he turned to face her. "I will not accept a defeated one or a loser as my wife, Erica." With those words, her heart plunged into despair until she felt him kiss her gently on the cheek. "But I will accept you as my wife, as long as you realize we both will make mistakes because of how new we are to each other."

Getting up, she grabbed one of his hands to guide him. "Gladly, my lord."

"Part of tradition is to call me 'my lord,' I take it?"

"Yes, at least for tonight. After that, we'll see. Centaurian men get off on that kind of thing." Walking away from the fire he had started, Erica led them to the back of the tree which couldn't be seen by the citizens of Yanapeachu, where a small stable stood.

"Erica, before we go through with this, I want you to repeat something I am about to say."

"Certainly."

"'I am not a loser, I am not a defeated one, but I give you myself as your wife freely.' I want you to say those words, if you mean them, Erica."

Saying those words, she confirmed to him that she meant it. As they entered the stable, she took a moment to grab a towel from her bags to wipe off the makeup she had put on earlier. Looking around, she saw his bike was already here, and she shuffled her hooves nervously. "Not the honeymoon suite, I know…"

"It's fine," he assured her. Bringing his face to hers, forehead to forehead, they started to kiss passionately. In an almost absentminded manner, their bags were thrown into one corner. Whispering between kisses, Erica asked him, "Know that sweet, sugary smell you've been smelling on and off all day?"

"Yes," he whispered back.

"It's been me, and my desire to be with you like this."

"So, I'm marrying a horny horse woman?" he asked, teasing her between kisses.

"And a pure one, part of tradition is that, until we marry, we try to not even masturbate."

Reaching down to his shorts, she undid the button and zipper holding them up, letting them hit the floor. Andrew deftly stepped out of them and kicked them into a corner. As he did this, Erica looked down to steal a glance at her future husband's penis, already semi-erect in his brief-style underwear, the head peeking out from the waistband. As it grew, she could see it was already leaking precum, getting into Andrew's underwear. Erica couldn't help but very gently giggle, saying, "Looks like I am not the only eager one here."

Andrew stepped back for a moment to take off his shoes and socks, and realized how soft the ground felt in the stable. Looking at Erica, he couldn't help but wonder how he got so lucky. For a moment, he saw fear in her eyes as she tried to cover up her breasts, starting to back up a bit. "Erica, is everything all right?"

"It's your..." she said, pointing to his penis that had now swelled so much it was well over the waistband of his underwear. "And it's my other half, it wants you so badly, and I am afraid I can't control it, even while I want you up here with me." She used her arms to emphasize her human half.

Slowly and calmly, he approached her, kissing her so gently on the lips she wasn't even sure they were kissing. "Don't worry, Erica. I am here for you, and I care for you. I want you to be as comfortable about all this as possible," he said, using a hand to indicate the two of them. Hearing his voice sounding friendlier, he added, "After all, in a sense, you started all this."

"I did at that, didn't I."

Despite less than a day of knowing him, Erica knew Andrew meant every word he said. Somehow she knew that he would battle from the pits of hell to the tops of the highest peaks for her safety. How had she gotten this lucky was a mystery to her that she didn't question at this time.

Pushing her up against a wall, Erica felt herself melting in his arms as her human half gained more control, easing the nerves of her horse half. She wasn't a filly anymore, and when lesser men would've run in fear or disgust, Andrew was still standing (literally, and figuratively) with her.

How many humans would've seen her and her people as monsters? In movies, humans were always running in fear whenever something Non-Human appeared.

Removing his hands from her back, she felt one hand trail up to her lips where she kissed them. Trailing those fingers down her blouse, and along her horse half as he made his way to her tail, it felt like raw electricity as he withdrew from her front and went to her rear. Lifting her tail up to invite him to plunge his penis into her, she was surprised as she felt one of his hands at work. She knew she wasn't built like human women, and she hoped he didn't have to ask which hole she wanted him in. That would be so embarrassing, but it wasn't like there were videos online of humans fucking centaurs. Her fears of embarrassment vanished as he started to run his hand up and down the length of her vagina. It felt like he had found the right hole, but it seemed like he was still looking for something, and it was driving her wild.

Buckling a bit, she started to lose herself in pleasure, and then it got better. He had found what he was looking for—a small section of flesh right above where he would put his penis. He put his thumb on it, and started to move it in a circle, and as he did, Erica felt pleasure like she could never have imagined, or even knew was possible.

With each movement of Andrew's thumb, it seemed the raw pleasure was compounding. It was getting stronger by the second, as was her urge to faint from what he was doing to her. Her eyes rolled into the back of her head, all she saw was white, and just when it couldn't seem to get any better, she exploded. Virginal fluids exploded from her, covering his hand as she panted. She wanted Andrew to be up here, touching her, feeling her, instead she felt denied him in a sense given he was with her horse half. She wished Andrew was up here near her human half, since she wanted to reward him for this experience. Then her horse half felt what it had wanted for years, but tradition had denied her—the tip of Andrew's penis as it slowly parted her vagina's lips and made its way slowly into her.

He wasn't being rough with her like a Centaurian man would be, he seemed so gentle as he eased his penis into her, sometimes even taking the time to pet her to reassure her everything was all right. With each thrust into her, he went a bit deeper, and another wave of pleasure hit her. Until she felt her hymen break, and, though she felt a twinge of pain, the pleasure he was giving her almost covered it up entirely. If Andrew felt anything negative about the small amount of blood leaking from it, he never said a word as he kept pounding her. It was as if breaking her hymen unleashed Andrew's own inner beast as he pounded her with a ferocity she could never have imagined. Each time his penis went in and out of her, it wanted to hang on as long as possible. She could feel the sweat running down her flanks the longer he kept penetrating her as she built up to orgasm. She wondered how he could hang on so long, but then again, it seemed like she had waited forever for this event, and been at it twice as long.

Fearing she couldn't hang on any longer, she whispered between pants, "Andrew, I am ready."

She didn't know if he'd heard her, but she felt him explode within her, filling her with his seed. She wouldn't be surprised if it all reached her womb as he did so. As he filled her with his seed, she felt her whole body, from head to hoof, experience an orgasm. Who knew the centaur body could experience the kind of pleasure he had given her tonight? He seemed to linger for a few moments, still ejaculating in her even though it felt like nothing more was coming out. As she lowered herself to the ground, she could still feel their combined fluids in her vagina slowly leaking out.

Andrew joined her in the front, bringing a blanket with him. Placing the blanket over them, he picked up and held Erica's hand before he got down and started to snuggle with her. "Hello, my wife," he said.

"Hello, my husband," she replied. He didn't know the joy it gave her to hear him say those three simple words. She kissed him on the cheek.

Looking at her breasts as he started to settle in, he said, "I am going to want to see those one day," as way of commenting on the fact she still had the remains of her blouse and sports bra on.

"I know," she said, yawning. "Just like I want to see yours," she continued sleepily, commenting on the fact that he still had his own black t-shirt on. They both knew of couples who had gone at it longer on their first night as a married couple, but given how they had both run a race, they were sexually satisfied. Snuggling together, they fell asleep, hand in hand.

Chapter 3

Sabrina backed her compact car into her reserved spot at the Centaur Café head office. Citing she would never need it, Erica had assigned her the spot when she had hired Sabrina as her executive assistant several years ago. It had taken her ages to find a compact car that would accommodate her Lamian build that she could drive, but it was so worth it. She had no desire or need for anything larger, and the car was so warm in the winter, which was a benefit it had over public transit that had always felt cold to her. By traveling by car, it also enabled her to maintain her polished look.

Sliding into the office, Sabrina caught a look at herself in the automatic glass doors. Long, silver hair that was as straight as an arrow framed her face, and hung to where her human half's back ended in the rear. Half-rim glasses where they should be, her silver earrings lined up from smallest to biggest until they reached the end of her ear lobes. It was all part of her effort to cultivate a very stylish, professional look. In fact, sometimes—in her tailored suits versus Erica, who one time met a supplier in just a sports bra—people assumed she ran the business.

But no, Sabrina reflected, some people were meant to be leaders, to forge something from nothing, and some were just excellent second-in-commands like she was. Slithering into the office, she was grateful she was working for a Centaur over another species. Generally, the non-human bottom species tended to make their work spaces bigger when they ran the business. There were laws in how large spaces had to be, but the bottom line was that if you paid for space, you could honour the letter of the law and not its spirit. She knew she was the first one in, given how it was summer and the heat always woke her up, but she knew of one person who was always here.

Looking up at a rather large air duct, she said, "What's the word, Archie?"

Sliding down on a silk strand from the duct, a rather devilish Arachne faced Sabrina upside down. It looked like he hadn't bothered to wash or style any of his hair in ages. Taking a moment, he flexed out all of his furry legs. Blinking all six of his eyes, he yawned, "You rang, madam?"

Sabrina gave a sidelong look to a flat screen TV which displayed different people, and the outcome they were betting on. Everyone knew the office betting pool, and knew what events could trigger it. It was one of the ways Erica had tried to make working at the Centaur Café more fun. Given some of the labour problems everyone faced, it was cheaper than giving everyone a raise. "Spill it. Last night before sunset all we had on was the race."

"Oh, that, right." He scratched his head absentmindedly before putting both hands behind it. "No word yet on the outcome, and the mountain is still shut down per Centaurian rituals. No one is let in or out."

Looking at the screen again, one name caught her attention. "You don't think Ruby was right, do you?" she asked.

"No way. Been what, seventy years since a human male came to our side? Fifteen since a female did it, and that was a Native American woman who married a merman out near James Bay. She got the work done to live under the sea, end of story." Despite being Canadian, Archie, for reasons no one asked about, always spoke with a Californian surfer's accent.

"True."

"Besides, I did my research on this Andrew cat. He is deep in human-ville, and the side bet I had with Ruby would kill me if she won."

Intrigued, Sabrina raised a silver eyebrow as she asked, "Side bet?"

"Yup. If I am right, I get all the death by fudge brownies I can eat for a year from Ruby."

"And if she's right that Andrew marries Erica and becomes one of us by marriage?"

Sounding dejected, he said, "I am her personal twenty-four seven IT guy for a year."

Chuckling, Sabrina said, "Ouch. I know Ruby has sometimes blown up tech by looking at it."

"I know, which is why I made the bet. I figured I had good odds on winning, but now...now the old spidey sense says I've been had."

Sliding away with a flick of her silver tail, Sabrina said to the chain's IT person, "Nothing you can do now, Archie, except wait and hope Ruby was wrong."

Giving a mocking salute to the departing Lamian, he said, "Too true, oh fearless boss lady until the real boss returns." With that, he went back up the silk strand to the office he had made in the air vents when he had been hired as the tech support guy for the company.

****

With a yawn, Andrew woke up, and the first thing he saw were Erica's breasts right in front of him, still in her blouse and sports bra. With a kiss to his head, she said, still sounding a bit sleepy, "Good morning. I guess we both slept in. Makes sense, given how long our day was yesterday." Her voice sounded almost musical to him.

Stretching his arms with another yawn, he got up, and everything came flooding back to him from the day before, a simple day which ended in a most unusual way. As he had slept, he had marked it all off as him being overworked, or a ride that had gone on too long. After all, there were plenty of mountain bikers who swore they saw things in the deep woods, but were only figments of imaginations. However, laying before him was a woman who was half human, and clearly half horse, and if his memory was correct, she was now his wife, according to her people's traditions.

During this time, he hadn't said a word, so Erica chose to break the silence. Looking down at herself as she played with her hands in a nervous manner, she said, just barely loud enough for him to hear her, "So...I was thinking. Technically, we haven't completed the ceremony, and we both got caught up in things. I am willing to let you out, or you can always reject me still, given how I lost the race." Despite not knowing her that long, Andrew could hear a sadness in her voice.

With his cock half erect, he slowly walked towards her, looking down at her and trying to catch her eyes. His voice was barely a whisper. "Is that what you want? A one-night stand? A chance to say you were with a human, and let me go along my merry way?"

"It's not about you, and it is. Humans aren't generally attracted—" She stopped mid-sentence as his penis touched her nose. Her eyes shot up. "Oh."

Smiling, he responded, "Yes, 'oh' indeed." Very firmly, looking her in eyes that were now looking up at him, he asked, "Do you want out?"

"No."

"Good. But I think, just for good measure, you need something this morning."

"Oh?"

Walking behind her, he said, "I am going to fuck you until you are so sore you can't walk for a few days." With a wink, he continued, "You can call your manager. Tell that person you need a few days off, but I want there to be no reason you'll doubt the fact that I accept your people's tradition, and I now want you as my wife."

"Naturally, my husband," raising her tail, the smell of her eagerness for sex began to fill the air. Knowing what he did now, Andrew's penis went from light morning wood to full hard-on. Lining up with her vagina, he was just about to start making love to her when the sound of someone clearing their throat interrupted them.

"Ahem."

Walking into the stable came a woman who had the ears of a wolf, and a red, bushy tail that ended in a white tip which seemed to come out from just above her lower back—it looked like that of a fox. Each step she took seemed to scream sex, given how it appeared her white t-shirt, and jeans were practically painted on. Looking down at her feet, Andrew saw that, instead of feet, she had a strange combination of feet and paws. Because of the claws, he could hear a soft clicking with each step she took. Her green eyes flashed as she looked at Erica, saying, "Been a while, Erica."

For the first time since Andrew had known her, Erica actually sounded angry as she got up, which made her a few inches taller than their uninvited guest. "Been a while indeed."

Challenging Erica, the woman said, "Maybe you should introduce me to your man? After all, he will need to know my name when I win the challenge and claim him as mine."

"Andrew, meet Alexis—owner of the Foxtrot Café chain. She might not look it, but technically, she's a werewolf."

Ever since waking up to find Alexis here, Andrew had looked around in vain for his shorts, and his attempts to cover up his manhood with his hands weren't doing the job while trying to act like this was normal, which it was far from. "Aren't werewolves supposed to change more, and during a full moon?" he asked.

"Given how long it's been since humans had any real contact with our people, some of the information is"—Alexis paused for a moment to find the right words—"out of date." Bringing her tail up, she gave it a quick rub, "Besides, I couldn't imagine looking like normal human for most of the time."

"If you couldn't imagine it, then why challenge for one?" Erica asked sternly.

Despite his odd position behind Erica, Andrew raised his hand. "I am wondering, what is this challenge you two are talking about?"

Alexis started to walk towards them as she responded. "Due to the limited amount of men in our population, women have the right to challenge for a man as he chooses his first wife." Stopping not three feet from them, Alexis bounced her chest, which Andrew figured offhand had to be double-D cups at least. Continuing, she said, "Then again, maybe your human doesn't want a Centaur? Maybe he wants a wolf instead? If he chooses me over you, then I see no need for combat."

Andrew knew he was going to have to ask Erica about this "first wife" bit later. Getting out from behind her, he glared at Alexis as he said, "I don't know the rules of your challenge, but I want you out of here. Now!" There was something in his voice that said he would broker no disagreement on this.

Looking him over, Alexis licked her lips in approval. "Nothing to be ashamed of down there, and full of fire in your belly. I like! When I claim you as mine, you'll make me some fine cubs!"

"Leave now!" he countered.

"Make me!" Ignoring Andrew, she charged at Erica, throwing the first punch only to find Andrew as he blocked her path.

Erica watched as Andrew's body language shifted from trying to preserve his modesty—given how he still didn't have any pants on—to someone ready for a fight. Moving on the balls of his feet, hands up near his face, but not close enough so they could be used against him, he seemed ready to counter every move Alexis made. "Wrong move, wolf!" he snarled.

On one hand, Erica was deeply offended, since he was breaking tradition. On the other, she couldn't help but realize how right she was when she had read his Qi, his life force. She had known of people who could read it deep enough that they knew strangers as if they had been together their whole lives. As her mother had taught her, words were good, but Qi rarely, if ever, lied.

Andrew and Alexis circled each other before Alexis made the first move, which, incidentally, was the wrong one. She threw a simple round-house punch, which Andrew countered by dodging. Grabbing her extended arm, he threw her towards one of the stable walls. Hitting a wall, she was disoriented for a few moments, and in those moments, he leapt at her. Spreading his legs, he was on top of her, forcing his forearm on her throat. "Yield!" he shouted, keeping the pressure tight as he held her to the floor.

Spreading her arms out, she slammed them to the floor. With fire in her eyes, she replied in submission, "Done."

Both of them got up, and Alexis brushed herself off. "Nice trick," she said to Andrew before addressing them both. "All right, since I see you are willing to fight for your right to be with her, I yield the right to be First Wife, but this isn't over." As she left, she threw Andrew one last taunt over her shoulder. "Oh, yeah, have fun descending the mountain without your shorts and underwear, human."

Behind Andrew, Erica couldn't help but smile as she looked around the stable to confirm Alexis' statement. While her and Andrew had been sleeping, Alexis must've snuck in, removed Andrew's shorts and underwear before making her grand entrance once they woke up. It was true to the Wolf part of her—always having a trick up her sleeve. She knew why Alexis wanted the role of First Wife, just like she knew her rival wanted to run the largest café chain among the Non-Humans. With Andrew at her side, it was possible humans would soon see Centaur Cafés pop up in their world also.

Walking over to her saddle bags, she retrieved the heart-shaped locket from one of them. Closing her eyes for a moment, she couldn't believe that it was finally happening. Ever since earning the right to be First Wife over ten years ago, she had dreamed of this day. Holding the locket up to her heart, she gave a sigh that spoke of pure, unadulterated bliss.

Behind her, she heard Andrew say, "I am sorry if I might not be in the mood, Erica. I don't like to fight."

Turning around to face him, she said, "It doesn't matter. What matters is that despite Alexis calling on one of the traditions among our people, you fought and defeated her. It was not your role according to tradition to do so, but you did so anyways." Looking him in the eyes, she called on every ounce of sincerity she could muster. "You are a man I would be honoured to call my husband and lord, even if you weren't human." Changing her tone of voice, she asked, "Remember how you asked about this locket?" She held it up for him to see.

"Yes?"

Opening it up for him to see, it held several gold rings with diamonds in them. She pulled one out as she took his right hand, saying, "I, Erica of the Centaurs, take thee, Andrew of the Humans, to be my husband and lord, from now until the end of our natural lives." She glided the ring down one of his fingers. She then took a second ring and placed it in his free hand, letting the locket fall back to her chest. "I need you to say precisely what I am about to say." He nodded, and she recited to him, "'I, Andrew of the Humans, take thee, Erica of the Centaurs, to be my First Wife, and lady, from now and until the end of our natural lives.'"

She held up her left hand to him. He repeated what she had just said as he slid the ring onto the proffered finger. Andrew noticed how both rings seemed to be thicker than traditional wedding bands, almost as wide as those given to champion sports teams. Without anyone touching the rings, he watched in wonder how, in seconds, a crude approximation of a centaur was carved into one side of his ring, as a human joined the other. The same process happened on Erica's ring.

Smiling, she said, "It is done." She began to look a bit panicked. "It also means we have an hour to vacate the mountain."

"So, we're one hundred and ten percent officially married now? No need for priests, town officials, nothing like that?"

Erica closed up the locket and placed it in the saddle bags. "Nope, no need. Because of how different species become married, it's normal for our rings to have nanotech in them that record the marriage for us."

Grabbing his socks and shoes, Andrew replied, "That's why you used the word 'thee,' it's a trigger word?"

Putting on her saddle bags over her rear end, she tossed Andrew his backpack. "Precisely."

Opening it up, he found his wallet and keys inside of it. Clearly Alexis wasn't totally cruel, despite her apparent adverse relationship with Erica. "And the hour?"

"Normally this is a public park, but, like other public locations, if a species' traditions need the land, it takes precedence over the needs of the public. Everyone knows this, so they tend to clear out fast when it happens. In fact, Alexis could be in trouble for what she did, if we chose to press charges."

Securing the bag to his back, Andrew looked Erica over, and wondered how his life had gone from so mundane to so different. Less than a day ago, he was a happy bachelor who worked from a home office doing different jobs in the field. Now, he was married to a woman who was half human, half horse, and he had fought a woman who was a werewolf. He smiled—there are always new places to discover, he thought, it just depends on where you go.

"What are you thinking?" Erica asked him as they exited the stable, hand in hand.

"Just how my life has gone from normal and boring, to something I couldn't have expected twenty-four hours ago."

Smiling, she said, "You know, one day I am going to have to see how you got out here, and say a prayer or something at that spot, since fate did shine on me that day."

Correcting her, he said, "On us, you mean." He hugged her with one arm as he stood beside her.

As he got to his bike, he felt a bit self-conscious walking it naked, but Erica assured him Non-Humans weren't as likely to judge him for being naked, especially given how he was with her. Any public official likely to punish him for being naked would check public records first, see he'd just been married to Erica and let them go on their way without even stopping them.

Walking down the mountain, hand in hand, Erica assured him they would make it down in time; she knew ways out of the park where they would avoid being seen by the public, though some would be disappointed.

"Where to after this?" Andrew asked. "I know I will be arrested if I return to my apartment naked. Someone will see me along the way. As for you," he said, smiling at the thought of the modern world finding out about her, "you'd be on the front screen of every smartphone, tablet, and TV in seconds."

"Because I am a Centaur?"

"No, because of how beautiful you are."

With that, she gave him a kiss on the cheek. "Can I keep you?"

He could hear the playfulness in her voice. "I think that can be arranged."

Keeping her eyes on the trail ahead, she replied, "Seriously, the next stop for us is my—" She swiftly corrected herself, continuing, "*Our* home. It doesn't have any furniture designed for humans, but within a few days we'll be set up."

"I can't wait to see it."

Walking in silence, they enjoyed the walk down the mountain. It wasn't like the race up it, where Erica was panicking a bit inside that she'd lose no matter what, while Andrew was racing to prove that despite his machine being designed to go down mountains, it could go up them just as well. At the time, he had just been hoping his prize would be what that locket meant, and seeing Erica out of her costume.

Chuckling at his naïveté, he knew it would take time for him to adjust to the new reality. Getting to the bottom of the hill and entering the woods, Erica assured them they were safe. Animals tended to avoid Non-Human territory, just like they avoided humans, unless they were hungry. Andrew finally asked her one of the big questions that had been nagging at him since they became married.

"You and Alexis both mentioned 'First Wife.' What does that mean?"

Erica knew that polyfidelity was not normal in North America, if not most of the world. It was one of the reasons why getting humans to join them was hard, even when both species met accidently. She hoped Andrew was one of the more flexible minds out there, and not one to believe in one man, one woman, otherwise she was going to be in trouble with some of her oldest and dearest friends. "Due to birth ratios, we practise polyfidelity."

"How do birth ratios affect the fact that you practise group marriages?"

"On average among all our people, for every male birth, there are eight to twelve females born. It depends on the species, and it's been like this for five hundred years."

"So, not a short-term problem. Pollution as the cause is off the table, since that is relatively new."

"Precisely. Up until about four hundred and seventy-five years ago, we practised marriage like your people did. However, we saw the birthing trends, and realized we had to change to keep people happy."

"I assume it's eight women to one man?"

"No, actually its nine. There are exceptions granted sometimes by the High Council, our highest governing body, or the racial leadership if it's a 'pure' marriage. The first wife and husband have the most say in the marriage. Each of them can normally bring up to three women into the marriage. The last spot is reserved for a woman who either both want to bring in, or for one who purchases her way into it."

"Must be kind of humiliating if you need to purchase your way into a family, like saying you only love me for my money."

"It is, trust me. It is done very rarely for a reason, even rarer for men to purchase their way into a family, or to start one that way."

Stopping their walk, Erica looked Andrew straight in the eyes, and took one of his hands and put it against her chest. "Andrew, I want you to understand that I will not force you into a group marriage, but I do have friends who I promised I would help find a husband through me. They actually paid for the locket and the rings inside of it. The reason they asked me to seek a husband for them is because Centaurs are known for being ultra selective with their men. That race we did was meant to test you both mentally and physically. I am willing to face the consequences alone if you reject them before meeting them."

Gently taking his hand away from her chest to help keep him from getting too excited, he asked, "Do I have the right to reject them if I don't like them, after meeting them?"

"Naturally, just like I can reject anyone you want to bring in, but only we can do it, since we founded this clan."

Resuming their walk, he asked, "Clan?"

"Depending on the races involved, clan is our general term to describe a common family unit of our people. If it was a family of bird hybrids, you'd have a flock, horse hybrids, you'd have a herd, and so forth."

"All right, and the others. What if they don't like someone we want to bring into our family, or what if they don't like me?"

"Well, if they don't like you, they can always forfeit their money and walk away. Given how we are inviting them into the family in the first place, everyone tends to get along. It's not like we're going to force the other women to sleep together. Unlike you, who does have the obligation to sleep with all of them at least once."

Andrew didn't know if that was good or bad luck, being obliged to sleep with all those women. "But that is why I have the veto power, and you have it because...?"

"It is how we honour the past, when we had marriages that humans have now. This way, the original wife didn't feel jaded by her husband sleeping with other women. In a sense, the idea of three a side came from the old days with various friends from both the groom's and bride's side."

Erica let out a sigh of contentment as they breached the trees before entering a clearing where Erica's small, white house stood. "Welcome to our home, my husband." Turning to him, she asked him to close his eyes, which he did. Leading him behind the house, she took his bike from him and took off his backpack along with her own bags. Andrew could hear something mechanical starting up when Erica told him to open his eyes. To his surprise, he saw a fully functional in-ground hot tub. "I know we have to do other things," Erica said, kissing him full on the lips, "but I am hoping you'll let me properly welcome you to our home for the first time before we get to work."

"As you wish, my wife. We both deserve a goodie."

She could read him a mile away at moments like this. She whispered, "I like that word, 'goodie.' What kind of goodie do you want?"

Not asking her permission as their lips were interlocked, he violently ripped the remains of her white blouse open in one pull, throwing it aside onto the grass. With expert skill, he managed to undo her black sports bra, and she grabbed his shirt as he backed up. Both now naked, they felt each other completely as they continued to kiss naked in the forest, her forest. Erica owned a little over a square kilometre of land that they now stood on. Even then, there was distance between her neighbours.

Despite some extra weight on him, Erica could feel the muscles on his chest. *Good*, she thought, *he's not unfamiliar to working out.* Now she was torn on what she wanted them to do next.

Between kisses, as their tongues explored each other's mouths, she pulled back and commanded him by saying, "Mount me, NOW!"

Backing up, she knew Andrew would assume she wanted to feel his penis inside of her, and she did, but not yet. She grabbed his hand as she lowered herself. "Ride me!"

As Andrew got on top of her, Erica felt an erotic energy coursing through her she didn't know was possible. "But we're—" Andrew began to protest, but Erica cut him off.

"Don't worry, where we are going, no one will care if we are naked." Placing his hands under her breasts, she commanded, "Just do as you feel like, don't worry about anything, and leave the rest in my hands, my love."

With that, she took off. She knew these woods like the back of her hands. It felt magnificent—her black hair blowing back, and her shorter, brown horse hair also joining it. She could feel Andrew's fear coursing through him as he hung on tight, and she hoped this would be temporary. Surely enough, it was as he began to loosen up.

Feeling his way up her breasts, she wondered briefly if this is what human women felt like when they were in the missionary position, where they felt every square inch possible of their mate. Feeling his hands run up and down her breasts, it was like pleasure she had never experienced before. She was going to have to get those hands insured, she thought as he continued to play with them. Suddenly, both hands stopped playing with her breasts as she picked up speed again. One of them broke away to take one of hers and gently guide it towards his semi-hard penis. The other, to turn her head to kiss him. Despite where their lips were, she kept one eye where they were running; she had lived here for years, and knew it like the back of her hand, but unexpected things had been known to happen before. This was living, she thought, and she knew if anyone was behind them, they'd see the trail of fluids the both of them were leaving in their wake, as his pre-cum rolled down her side, and her vagina kept leaking lubricant also, so thick it was almost visible to even a blind person. The Centaur she was before last night would've been embarrassed, but the one she was now didn't care one bit.

Satisfied now that her hand was where he wanted it, Andrew brought his hands up to her breasts. He could feel her nipples grow harder the more he massaged them. She seemed eager to kiss him harder, to the point where their teeth hit several times. Despite the intensity of how he was making her feel, her hand on his penis was so gentle as it went from rubbing his ball sack to his inner thighs. Each time she touched him, it was electric. He could feel his penis grow larger with each time she touched him down there; he so wanted to get off of her and in her.

Opening his eyes for a moment, she read what he wanted to do, and her eyes said no, so he had one place left to go with this. As her hand expertly massaged the tip of his penis, he did his best to hold back his orgasm, even as he lost control of his hands on her breasts. *Where did she learn to do this?* he wondered moments before his vision went white; she removed her hand from his penis just as it covered her back with semen in several shots. Right at that moment, with him hanging on, she reared up on two legs, and he felt her explode beneath him in several back-to-back orgasms.

Releasing his grip on her, he slid down her back, along with some of his semen, and while she was still rearing up, he slammed his hard penis right into her vagina, even as she was coming. Just like the story of the little boy with the dike in Holland, he temporary stopped this flood. He couldn't see her face, but he knew her eyes were rolling in the back of her head with pleasure as she stammered out the word, "H-h-h-h-husband!"

Getting a firm grip on her rear, he kept focus on his goal—to stay as hard as possible as he pleasured his new wife. With each thrust, he could feel it becoming more wet in there, more inviting. It wasn't like last night when he deflowered her, it wasn't as tight. He could feel her heartbeat each time he slammed his penis into her, and with each thrust, she was letting out a moan of pleasure. Neither one knew how long it lasted until they both orgasmed at the same time. He saw their combined fluids leaking out of her, and she lay down in the long grass. He had been so distracted by what she had wanted, he didn't realize that, in all her running, she had taken them to a small glade that was within eyesight of their home.

Looking down at her, she seemed so happy as she cupped her breasts and lay back in the tall grass. Only now could he see her sides were streaked with sweat, as was her hair. Playfully, she removed one arm from her breasts, and used one finger to touch the tip of his penis. "Someone did good work today." Seeing it starting to harden a bit, she continued, "And he looks ready to play again."

Joining her on the ground, he wrapped his arms around her, making sure to grab her breasts. "And I want to spend more time playing with these."

Giggling as Andrew played with her breasts, Erica responded, "You're as bad as a foal with those."

Adjusting himself, Andrew lay his head on one of her massive breasts. With the need to sleep after sex kicking in, sleepily he said, "How about we cuddle for a while, then get some breakfast before taking on the rest of our first day as a married couple?"

Smiling, Erica kissed him on the head. "Done, but if I wake up first, I will wake you up with a blow job."

Together under the blue sky, under the shade of the trees, they fell asleep.

****

A shrill female voice shouting, "Erica Swifthoof, what in the name of the gods do you think you are doing with that—with that—with that human!" is what woke both Erica and Andrew from their light nap. Snapping awake, they saw a pair of Centaurs before them, and the difference in them were night and day. The shorter of the pair shared Erica's Asian ancestry. She was shouting, still in a fury as she raised her arms up and down, and her round face became as red as a tomato with every moment.

The other woman, a blonde, grabbed her arm, addressing her firmly. "Mrs. Swifthoof, calm down!"

Still shouting at the top of her lungs at what kind of degenerate her daughter was, seducing a human of all things, and didn't care about their laws, their traditions. How no Centaurian man would even look at her because she had slept with a human. Firmly grabbing onto Mrs. Swifthoof's arms, the other woman said, "Mrs. Swifthoof, look at their hands!"

Glaring at the blonde Centaur, the shorter Asian woman shook her long, brown hair. "Why should I look at their hands you, you stupid cop! My daughter should be arrested! That human needs his memory wiped! Now!"

Adjusting her blue hat with one hand, the other centaur repeated herself, glaring at the shorter woman. "Please, ma'am, look at their hands."

"I called the Yanapeachu Police to help find my daughter, and here she is, naked as a bird, with a—a human!" The word "human" came out as if she'd said something vile.

"And now that we are not ten feet from them, you won't arrest her!"

The blonde woman's blue eyes turned as firm as ice. "I will not repeat myself. Look. At. Their. Hands!" Each word was a statement unto itself.

Forcing herself to calm down, Mrs. Swifthood muttered something about calling her council member, but did as instructed and looked at the couple's hands. In an instant, her face went from as red a tomato to as white as a ghost, and she said, "Oh."

"'Oh,' indeed!" Slamming a front hoof on the ground so hard Andrew and Erica felt it, the officer continued, "We do not arrest married people for being naked, or appearing to have had sex on land which one of them owns!"

With her jaw seemingly still on the floor, Mrs. Swifthoof put her hands together before her face, and bowed down to the ground, saying, "Most honourable daughter, and honourable Human son-in-law, you honour the Swifthoof clan with your union. Please accept my deepest apologies, I did not expect to find out you had become married in the last week, Erica. Much less to a human."

With one hand, Andrew tried to cover his penis as he got up, while using the other one to help Erica get up. Though gritted teeth, Erica said to her mother, "You are forgiven, Mother." She stretched the word "mother" out into two clear syllables, her only means of expressing how she felt.

Sensing the tension between the three people, the officer cleared her throat. "Look, maybe—" she started before turning to Andrew, "Sorry, your name, please?"

"Andrew," he replied.

Continuing from where she'd left off, she said, "Maybe Andrew can find something to wear inside the house?" Andrew further tried in vain to cover his pride. "And maybe Mrs. Swifthoof can wait for him outside while he gets it?"

Getting up, Mrs. Swifthoof looked up at the officer. "A most wise idea, officer. It would a good idea to get to know my new son-in-law, and understand how he came to be among our people."

"Uh, I don't have a key yet to the house," Andrew protested with an embarrassed smile on his face.

Erica responded, "Oh, the house works on biometrics, and once we became married, you were cleared to enter the house."

Leaning over, he gave her an affectionate kiss on the cheek. "Thanks, Erica."

In front of the other women, she grabbed him by the shoulders, forcing him down into a deep kiss. Holding on for several moments as he relaxed, one of her hands went down towards his ass to pinch it. It was a clear sign that this was not an arranged marriage, and to show her ownership of him before the others. Once she was happy, she released him. "I'll see you later, my love. I want to talk with the officer for a few moments, okay?" With a cold glare she said, "Mother," effectively dismissing the other Centaur.

As both people walked away, a smile crossed the face of the blonde officer. Anyone who'd spent any time with her knew it was rare to see any kind of expression there while she was working. Playfully, she put a hand under one of Erica's exposed breasts to raise it. "Been a while since I saw these," she said, bending down and licking the other Centaur's dark nipple. "Maybe we could play a bit as your husband and mother get to know each other."

Smacking the officer's hand lightly, Erica replied with a haughty tone, "How about we say we did, and don't. After all, I am a married woman now." As she said this, she looked down at her ring and played with it a bit. "Still, it has been a while, hasn't it, Tiffany?"

She walked slowly towards the hot tub where Andrew and Erica's clothing was still thrown about. "Eight years of you dating different men and women, trying to find a good match," Tiffany reflected. "I know you gave into pressure from us years ago to give up on your dream."

There was a silence between the two friends before she continued, "But, I've got to give you your dues, you originally wanted a human, ideally a male, and you landed one in the end." Holding up her hand to her mouth, she giggled lightly at the double meaning of the term. "How is he? Does he know what he faces ahead?"

Shaking her head, Erica replied, "He doesn't know about the political situation yet. He only knows that by marrying me he's legally allowed to know about us, and that he can still return to the human world. As per the other side, he's everything I wanted and more. When he took me last night, he was so gentle with me, and with the stuff he did to me." She could practically feel her body tremble with what they had just done earlier today.

She picked up her bra and the remains of her blouse—Erica was considering hiring someone to scour the mountain to find the rest of it—along with Andrew's shorts, and underwear. As she was about to put her bra back on, Tiffany's hand stopped her. "Don't, it's not like anyone here hasn't seen these before," she said, grinning from ear to ear. "So, in all seriousness, when do I get to meet him? It's not like he's got anything to hide."

Smiling, Erica responded, "Two weeks, nothing hardcore?"

"Try twelve hours, and I want to be ridden like you were."

"Tiffany, be reasonable, he's human. We know they are still sexually immature as a people. Heck, they barely accept bisexual, transgender, and homosexual people. Non-Human group marriages are going to be a bit to take in for him. I mean it's one thing to accept it on paper, it's another to get involved with one. We both know it's not easy."

Holding up her left arm, Tiffany used her right hand to finger a small, heart-shaped locket that hung off her wrist, "You know I could tell Jessica? Force the issue. She does not know you're married yet."

"That's blackmail, Tiffany. He hasn't even moved in yet."

"No, this is reality," Tiffany said sternly. "You earned the right to be a First Wife, and Lady. Some of your oldest friends agreed to be your wives and accept your choice of consort. Well, now that part one is done, time for part two."

Looking at Tiffany, Erica knew she was dead serious— she wasn't bluffing, she never did. "All right, best offer I'll make: three days, three nights. Let him move in, get his feet on the ground, then say a week of us collectively dating? No sex until he decides not to veto you per tradition, and you decide you want to stay."

Smirking, Tiffany said, "I put my faith in you to find him, what makes you think I don't want him?"

"Tiffany…" Erica warned.

Holding her hands up, she replied, "All right, I give. No sex until he's agreed not to veto me, per tradition. Mind you, if I wasn't on duty, and with your mom, I would've been tempted to give him a proper wake-up call." She licked her lips, continuing, "I so want to suck that big, fat lollipop he has between his legs."

Playfully whipping her sports bra at her friend, Erica said, "You can do that once he agrees *not* to veto you."

"How could he not want me? I am blonde, blue-eyed, run faster than the wind, and could support two to four foals on these," she said as she lifted her chest up to emphasize her rather large breasts that she knew were larger than Erica's own.

Walking alongside her friend to the other side of the house, Erica said, "Don't get me wrong, Tiffany, it's one thing to attract someone physically to you, but it's another for them to be there emotionally for you."

"And you know Andrew is emotionally there for you, how?"

"Since Alexis invoked the challenge, he took my place, and kicked her ass."

"That sounds like him being old school human. Isn't that a bad thing?"

"Normally I'd agree, but before Alexis challenged us, I gave him an out, and he didn't take it."

"He didn't?"

Shaking her head, she said, "Nope. He seemed determined to prove to me he was committed to us until Alexis showed up, and challenged me."

"All right, I am curious... What was he ready to do to you to prove he was committed to the marriage?"

With a wink, Erica replied, "Oh, you'll find out one day, if you are lucky."

****

Andrew had to admit that the last day had felt like one wild ride. He had heard from enough friends how odd it was to meet their partner's parents. To meet his new mother-in-law naked was not how he had planned it. Now he was standing on the front porch of his wife's home wearing a bright red Amazing Woman robe he had found in her closet. He was now trying to make small talk with the woman, his cheeks still a bit red from embarrassment over how they had met. "So, how do you do, Mrs. Swifthoof?"

Smiling, Mrs. Swifthoof extended her hand. "I believe this is how humans greet each other, no?"

Chuckling, he replied, "Actually, among family it's acceptable to hug one another, but I think given how poorly we know each other, a handshake will do fine." Grabbing her hand, he shook it firmly. "So, where do we start?"

"Was my daughter satisfactory in bed? I know you humans do not have the...social pressure to remain pure like we do."

Andrew's jaw dropped like a rock, and he started to laugh. "First you are upset for finding me naked with your daughter, now you're asking how your daughter was in bed? Is this normal for you people?"

Smiling, she replied, sounding as calm as possible, "Normal depends on how the individual perceives reality, no?"

"True."

"I am sure if you were to go home, tell your friends about your recent adventures, they'd say this is not normal. However, by your standards, this is normal?"

"I don't know if it's normal to me, but those who fail to adapt to reality often find themselves punished for ignoring it."

"True. I assume the more time you spend with our people, the more normal it will become for you?"

"Naturally. Mind if I ask you a question?"

"You may."

Pausing for a moment, Andrew tried to figure out which of a dozen questions he wanted answered. "Erica told me about the treaty limiting contact between our people. Is there any talk of that treaty being withdrawn?"

"None."

"Why not?" It was such a simple question, but he continued. "Based on the fact Erica all but jumped me, I suspect there is a high demand for humans among your people."

With a bit of a snarl in her voice, she replied, "Since you are not ready yet for first contact!"

"I am not ready for first contact? Me, personally?! I just married your daughter after knowing her for less than twelve hours."

"And you do not know what that means."

"So, I can learn."

Smiling smugly, she replied, "Yes, you can learn, and therein lies the problem."

"The problem being...?" Andrew felt like his mother-in-law was baiting him at every turn. Maybe this is why he had been a bachelor so long; he didn't want to deal with this.

"What percentage of the global population is ready for first contact? What percentage if they met another intelligence would treat it as an equal?" She raised her arms in rage. "How many humans treat humans as equal, and will treat one as a lesser for any one of a thousand reasons?!"

It dawned on him what she was talking about. "I see," he said, conceding to her point of view.

"Even now, despite the treaty, in much of the second, third, and fourth worlds, we are hunted like animals. We don't dare strike back, for fear of what would happen to us as a people if we openly broke the treaty."

"And even in the first world," Andrew commented, "there are zealots who would mark you as demons, or scientists who would demand you be examined in full detail, while subjecting you to inhuman experiments."

"And therein lies the problem. We are aware of individuals like you who will treat us like equals, but we are also aware of the other side of the coin. We dare not risk it, since we are so limited in numbers."

Countering, he asked, "What good is a treaty if your people are not equals under it?"

"You do have a point about how the treaty tends to be one way, but we don't have the numbers to challenge it." Ominously, she added, "Yet."

"But do you have the numbers to defend what is yours from those who would harm you?"

"That is for our leaders to say."

"I take it you are not a leader?"

Chuckling, she replied, "No, I am merely a second wife of my husband, and am employed as a physiotherapist for injured Centaurs. I never had as much ambition as Erica."

"And by your Clan name, it's safe to assume you are all Centaurs?"

"No, but everyone is equestrian in our family. I was close to my husband before the competition and might've been his first wife if I had won the right to be one. Erica did us all proud when she earned that right."

"Earned the right, so this isn't self-regulated?"

"By no means, that would be chaos. Everyone would claim to be first wife material."

"So, there is a little chaos on who gets to be in charge, and veto on another. Hardly end of the world."

Something in her smile told Andrew that there was more to this than he knew. "I am sure you'll learn in time what it means to be the head of a Clan, or a Herd if you should choose to only accept Centaurs or others like them as your wives."

With a bit of a smirk, he said, "Isn't it hard to be a Herd if I am human?"

"All things tend to be possible with our people."

Something in the way she said that unnerved him, but before he could dwell on it, he heard a familiar hoof-fall behind him. Before he could react, a hand grabbed his behind though the robe he was wearing, as another hand another drew him in for a kiss. Releasing him, Erica asked, "Mother keeping you busy?"

"We had an interesting discussion. It seems I have a lot to learn about your people."

Erica took a position to his right, and for some reason, the officer took a spot to his left. He could swear he could feel the officer trying to reach for his free left hand as Erica said, "Officer Tiffany and I spoke, Mother. Nothing more will be said of you interrupting us today. That being said, I think it'd be best if you went back to the city."

"Naturally, I assume you'll accept dinner on me, so we can get better acquainted."

"We'll see, odds are there is a lot of work for me to do back at the office," Erica said before giving Andrew a sly grin. "And there is a lot of work to do here as well."

"All right, I'll be in the city for a few days, please try to at least text me."

"I'll try, Mother."

Mrs. Swifthoof trotted away, leaving just the three of them at the entrance to Erica's house. Filling the silence, Andrew asked, "So, what's next?"

Turning to Andrew, Erica said, "I was serious. I do need to report to the office. Once I get dressed, I'll take off."

"Surely you can take some time off? Your boss can't be that much of a task master."

"Actually, she can be." Looking down at her hooves, she said, "Since I own the café we were at yesterday along with twenty-nine others like it."

"Oh."

She smiled meekly. "Forgive me?" she asked.

"Yeah, but before you go, maybe you could attend to one other problem?"

"Oh? What problem is that?"

It was at this point that Tiffany made a discreet exit, since clearly it was a problem for them as a married couple to attend to. She wasn't part of that family yet, but she suspected what they were going to do next.

****

For the first time as far as anyone could recall, Erica actually arrived work late. Not five to ten minutes I-had-to-stop-for-coffee late, but as in it was a little past one o'clock in the afternoon when she finally walked into the office. She had not even bothered to call in, as was her normal custom when she was running behind schedule.

As she made her way in, she gave a nod here, a smile there, before making her way to the center of the office where the betting pool results were displayed on one of the large flat screen monitors. *The more things change, the more they stay the same,* she thought, smiling. Looking up to an air vent, she said, "Archie, I need full holocam hook up, time to close up this pool. I want all cafés linked up with us. I also want to see the reaction from café twenty."

From the air vent, she heard, "Right-o, boss lady, we'll be live in five."

Erica pushed her hair back; she had done her makeup after her and Andrew had attended to that one other problem. Her body still tingled from the experience. Stepping into the circle of cameras that hung from the ceiling in the middle of the office, several of the office workers stopped what they had been doing to watch as Erica took her place. One of the advantages of a multi-camera shot was Erica did not have to worry about which camera to focus on. Without even a word from Archie, they lit up, and she knew she was on, just as she knew most of the cafés were now slowing down for a brief few moments to hear her announcement. "Good afternoon. As we are all aware, there is a betting pool going on regarding my love life. I admit, when I started these pools as a way to improve morale, I never expected to be the center of one."

Doing her best to remain calm, she chuckled a bit as she continued, saying, "I could give some long-winded speech about how business is doing, and how I am cancelling this pool, but I am not. Instead, I am going to let my hand do all the talking." Holding up her left hand clearly for all to see, she spread out her fingers so there was no obscuring the view of her ring. She could hear a moan from the air vent as she saw the pink-haired Ruby go nuts, running around café twenty when she revealed her wedding ring. Erica finished with a smile, "That's all, people. Pay the winners and get back to work."

With that, Archie killed the cameras recording her. She knew, depending on the café, countless different things were happening now. With the cameras shut down, the employees in the office rushed Erica to congratulate her on her marriage and ask about him. Those who lost the bet did not have any hard feelings, since it was so rare for a human to marry one of them. It was even rarer for it to happen after knowing one of them less than twenty-four hours, and to beat a Centaur at a marriage race was also extremely rare for any race.

After disengaging herself from her employees, she pushed back the wooden double doors to her office as she entered it. Several plants were spread out along the dark hardwood floor, and much to her surprise, there were a stack of envelopes from several courier companies on her desk awaiting her attention. The reason it was a surprise was that she tended to keep her desk clear, and she did everything via e-mail.

Sitting down at the other side of the desk, she was not surprised to see Sabrina had followed her in; what did surprise her, however, was the look on Sabrina's face. Around the office, she put up a good poker face, but when it was just the two of them, it was pretty hard for the Lamian to lie to her boss. Erica knew something had been wrong with Sabrina for a while. "What's wrong, Sabrina?"

Sabrina held up her left arm. Her wrist, where normally a small heart on a chain was, was now void. "I got vetoed a few days ago. My friend married a Yuki-Otoko, nice looking guy, ripped abs, but..."

Knowingly, Erica nodded her head as she said, "I see your point. We try to be as inclusive as possible as a people, but I know mating between a snowman and a Lamian would kill the Lamian since she or he is cold-blooded."

It was one of the areas where even the non-human antidiscrimination laws tended to end, if there were biological problems that caused the fight. Thankfully, most non-humans learned at a young age to control their respective non-human sides by the time they could do any real damage to each other besides name-calling. Or, in the case of a veto, no one felt offended since the one of the two involved would kill the other when they mated.

"If you want to talk about it, I'm here. Please feel free to take a seat," Erica said, indicating to the chairs before her.

"No, but I do have one more letter for you to read. My aunt sent it to me personally at the office, and asked I deliver it to you once you got in." Using the tip of her tail, Sabrina reached into her blazer and pulled it out before handing it to Erica. Without another word, Sabrina let herself out of Erica's office to resume her other duties.

On the back of the envelope that Sabrina had just handed her was the wax seal of the Head of the Lamian Council. It was a seal only used for official communications between council members or in the rare case where a head of one wrote a private citizen regarding official business. Despite the success of Centaur Café, Erica had never received one before. Using a letter opener, she opened it and started to read the letter.

Erica,

I bear you greetings from the Lamian Council, as the head of council. I apologize for seeming so informal during our first contact by addressing you by your first name. I do so since, as of the writing of this letter, you and your husband have not announced your clan's name. As you might be aware, my niece Sabrina is now free to become married, since she was rejected from a long-standing arrangement she had.

I understand you have space for one more on your own side of the clan, and countless women will be after your husband, given how he is human. On behalf of the council, I am authorized to offer ten million dollars as her bride price to buy in as our initial offer, but, naturally, this is subject to negotiations. We would also be willing to offer up political favors as well in lieu of money to help seal our bargain.

We both know the value of family and humans to our people, which is why even if you are reticent to wed Sabrina, maybe I can help introduce you to another lovely Lamian if you should be interested in having one in your clan.

I thank you for your time. Sabrina will be able tell you how to get in touch with me directly once you and your husband have discussed the situation.

Yours in Good Faith,

Madam Chancellor Zetus, Clan Xantang

Erica had no doubt of Zetus' sincerity, and she knew this was going to happen the second Andrew sealed their marriage this morning. She now strongly suspected that all the courier envelopes on her desk were from other leaders in the non-human world, and hackers who kept an eye on who married who. People who wanted a shot at something that happened so rarely—a human male marrying one of them.

Family and propagation were such a driving factor to her people; add the human element and the driving force expanded a thousand-fold. Putting the letter aside, she opened the next envelope. She strongly suspected it was going to be a long time before she got to actually work in the office. Maybe Andrew was right, maybe she should've called in sick today. She hoped he was having a better time with the integration office that was supposed to help him move, and answer any questions he had about non-humans.

****

Once everyone had left, Andrew had found some bed sheets in Erica's place, and had chosen to wear them as an improvised toga. Despite being assured by her that no one would care if he was naked, he cared. Just as promised, the doorbell rang at precisely 1:16 p.m. to the minute. He could admire a government agency with such accuracy.

Opening the door, he saw no one. Sticking his head out, he said, "Hello?"

"Down here!" said a gruff voice with a Brooklyn accent. Looking down, Andrew saw a small man with his black hair greased back in a ponytail. He was sticking his hand out. "Jerry of Gnome Express. We roam so you don't have to," the gnome said, clearly ending with his company's motto. "We're here to transport your stuff, as well as acclimate you and your electronics to our world."

Shaking Jerry's hand on instinct, Andrew looked around and said, "Where is your truck? How did you get out here?"

Rubbing his hands, the gnome replied, "Follow me and all will be revealed."

Following the gnome, he watched as one of the larger trees close to the house vanished, a metal plate appearing and in its place. "Hologram," the gnome explained. Stepping onto the plate as it descended into the ground, Jerry gave Andrew a sly grin and said, "You have no idea the amounts of money that are moving right now due to you, do you? Or the chaos you've caused for our people?"

"Why would me marrying Erica cause chaos among the gnomes, or cause money to be moved?"

Shaking his head, Jerry said, "Not chaos among the gnomes, among all the Non-Humans! Know that wedding race you did?"

"Yeah?"

"Well, it was recorded, and it is out there on our version of the net. It's given the ones who want the treaty gone food for thought on if it's time to break it."

Andrew's jaw hit the ground. "What! It was recorded! All of it?!"

Chuckling, Jerry said, "Don't get your undies in a bundle. Just the race part of it, part of Centaur Law. The naughty stuff they'll never record, and they have the muscle to put the fear into the most desperate paparazzi to enforce it."

"Why do they record it?"

"Just in case someone feels it was fixed towards either a win or lose. In the old days, blood told the tale. Now, recordings do the job. Frankly, I feel it's better this way—gives the couple a chance to think things out as they race. Helps with cold feet, and all that."

Down in what appeared to be a small garage, Jerry waved to three gnomes in the distance as they walked towards a van. "Those are my sisters," Jerry explained. "They are all single, so if they're a bit too friendly, I apologize."

Andrew continued, "You mentioned me giving the members of your society who want war second thoughts, mind explaining why?"

"Over the last hundred years or so, you humans have grown soft, especially this millennial generation!" Jerry spat as he said the word "millennial" in contempt. "Mark my words, the helicopter generation and the one to follow will be worse. Colouring books for adults, safety rooms in case you hear bad words in school! It's like you hid behind your mama's apron from birth to death, and whine like babies if things don't go precisely your way!"

"How did I give them food for thought again by marrying Erica?"

Muttering under his breath as his sisters charged them, Jerry said, "I'll explain in the van." Raising his voice, he continued, "Time for introductions."

Pointing to the one with green hair in pig tails, who wore a green dress that stopped just above her stocking-clad knees, Jerry said, "This is Bloom. She handles transportation of our biologicals."

"Hello," Bloom said, curtseying before making a feeble attempt to grab Andrew's ass, which he pushed away with annoyance.

Pointing now to the middle one wearing a blue jumpsuit with red hair that was standing on end, Jerry said, "This is Hotwire! She's our tech, never seen a busted machine she can't fix. She'll be handling the upgrading of all your tech."

Extending her hand, Hotwire said, "Put 'er there." Andrew shook her hand before Jerry pointed to the last one who was dressed completely in black from head to toe, contrasting starkly with her pale white skin. "This is Sherry, doubt she'll say much. She rarely does."

Raising her hand, Sherry waved it briefly.

"All right, ladies, let's load up and roll!" Jerry announced.

All three of the gnome sisters walked into the back of the van, while Andrew and Jerry entered the main cabin. "Where to first, Andrew?" Jerry asked.

"How about my car?"

"Done."

"Just one question," Andrew asked as Jerry put the van into gear. He looked straight ahead at the wall that appeared to be made of solid cement. "How did you get in here, and how do we get out?"

Smiling, the gnome gave the van's dash an affectionate pat, saying, "Simple interphasing matter transducer, built into the van for moves like this."

"A what?"

Turning to Andrew, Jerry said, "You stupid or something? Don't you know what an interphasing matter transducer is?"

"Until yesterday, I thought Centaurs, Gnomes, and countless other things like that were fictional, so I am still a bit new to this!"

"True. Know how between all atoms there is space?"

"Yup."

"An interphasing matter transducer lets us move though solid objects without it going 'boom,' part of the tech edge we have over you humans."

Flicking several switches before pressing hard on the gas, he suddenly cried, "And away we go!"

Andrew heard Jerry and his sisters behind them laugh as he was slammed into the seat from how fast the van was going. "No speeding rules?"

"Who needs 'em? When two interphasing objects intersect, they won't collide."

"Good point. You were saying about food for thought for the war-minded part of your people?"

Reaching into a small compartment built into the door beside him, Jerry withdrew a cigar. "You mind?"

"Nope."

Lighting the cigar from a lighter in the truck, Jerry took a puff before he continued, "You need to understand several things. The first being Centaurs are highly respected by all us non-humans, so if when they marry outside the family, so to speak, people take notice. Especially when it's a First Wife like Erica with her scores."

"Gotcha.'" Something more to learn about his new wife, Andrew thought.

Jerry took another puff off his cigar. "I've seen that leap you took over one of the rivers just before it becomes a waterfall. It took grit to push yourself up to full speed and make that jump."

"Why would me jumping over a river on my bike be considered having grit?"

"Since most millennials," Jerry said, spitting the word out again, "would have looked for an alternative route. Or they would've abandoned the bike, or the race! You took the path that took some stones. There were a few other moves that counted towards a higher score on your end. Given how you didn't know the full story at the time, people took notice."

"But Erica lied to me—there was no way to know I'd see her as a person after the truth came out."

"And if you declined, we wouldn't be here."

"Good point. So, showing a bit of courage and brains make them weak in the knees for me in a sense?"

"Bingo! Take a good, hard look at me, and guess how old I am," Jerry said, pounding on his own chest briefly.

Looking at the gnome through the slowly smoke-filling cabin, he guessed, "Forty to fifty years old?"

Laughing in response, Jerry said, "Turned one hundred and twenty-five last week."

"Congrats?" Andrew said weakly, totally unaware if that was a milestone or not for Jerry.

"Thing is, I've seen your people before they were your people. Yes, you have throwbacks all over the place for good and for ill. You, you might be like a fine machine we need more of, you've got a bit of old and new in you."

"What do you mean?"

Jerry adjusted some switches on the dashboard, which caused the van to rise from underground. Andrew half wondered how the motor ran without air if the entire thing was underground. Slamming on the brakes as the truck left earth, gravel stones and dust flew everywhere as they pulled into the parking lot. Jerry and Andrew left the cabin, and as Jerry passed the side of the van, he hit it. "Hotwire, you're up!"

"Yippie!" came from the van before the red-haired gnome leapt out of the back. Turning to Andrew, she asked, "You mind opening her up?"

Glad he had improvised a pocket in his toga, Andrew opened the car up via remote and watched as Hotwire pulled out his cellphone, placing it into her jumpsuit. Then, before anyone could say anything, she started to run around the car, placing some strange devices on each of the windows and throwing something onto the dashboard. Running towards the two men, she said, "Run!"

Before Andrew could ask what was going on, she grabbed both men's hands, almost pulling them behind the van by herself before yelling out, "Fire in the hole!"

There was strangely nothing—no shaking, no noise, nothing, like an unnatural silence. Hotwire then leads both Jerry and Andrew around the other side of the van where Bloom and Sherry await them. Looking on in horror, Andrew's jaw drops like a rock. "What did you do to my car?!"

Every window is now gone, as is the dashboard, but without any residual damage, inhuman in its precision. The cost to repair this easily exceeded the value of the car. Andrew was trying to imagine how he would explain this to his insurance company. Hotwire walked up beside him, sighing with contentment before saying, "I love this part of my job."

Barely holding back his anger, Andrew said, "Naturally, anyone would have fun blowing up other people's stuff."

Shaking her head, Hotwire said, "I didn't blow anything up; I used some precision micro-vacuum imploder devices to remove your windows and dashboard before I start upgrading your car."

"Precision micro-imploder devices?"

Guiding him towards the car, a work bench floated out from the van behind them. "Think of them like super strong vacuum cleaners where everything inside a designated space is sucked in, compacted, and prepared for recycling."

"Still, the point remains—you ruined my car."

Giving him a sideway glance, she replied simply, "And I plan to fix it, along with your cell phone." Pulling the phone out of her pocket, she held it by a finger and a thumb like it was something toxic. Pointing at the damaged screen, she asked, "What did you do, use a jack hammer on it?"

"It was on the repair list."

Placing the phone on the workbench she had retrieved from the van, Hotwire looked at it, saying, "This is why I never buy Korean, they don't know anything about the transparent metals. Might as well make a phone back in the dark ages given the tech they use." Holding up her hands in rage to emphasize how upset she was, she continued, "I mean, you humans don't even have holophones yet, and you call yourselves a sentient species!"

"Hey, sis, calm down," Jerry said before smacking Andrew affectionately, continuing, "Andrew here just buys the tech like everyone else. Question is, is it beyond hope?"

"I don't know," said Hotwire as she glared at the black smart phone. "Be almost criminal to repair such an arcane piece of technology, like restoring a stone knife, or a club." Sighing, she tapped on the workbench with one finger as she thought for a moment. "But I'll see what I can do. I'll work on this while my drones work on the car."

"Good, sis, thanks. How long do you think it will all take?"

"A few hours at most."

"Thanks, sis, you are the best." Turning to address his other two sisters waiting near the end of the van, Jerry yelled out, "Yo! Bloom, Sherry, load up, we're getting out of first gear back to Andrew's place."

Both gnomes replied, "Gotcha," and went running back into the van.

Getting back in the van and buckling up, Andrew said, "Jerry, I noticed that two of your sisters have unusual names, while you and another have normal ones. What's with that?" Looking in the side mirror as the van pulled away, Andrew continued, "Are you sure it's safe for Hotwire to be out there like that working?"

Taking a long drag from his cigar, Jerry replied, "Names with gnomes tend to evolve, sometimes with gnomes like Bloom, Hotwire, and I, after a while, we choose names we feel reflect who we are. While some like Sherry, despite her sunny disposition, sticks with the one our parents gave her."

"Hmm, good to know, and the Hotwire being exposed bit?"

Taking a tablet off the armrest that resided between the two of them, Jerry flipped it over to Andrew. "Typical procedures fell into place, including my hiring. It's all there, kid."

Opening up the tablet's screen, Andrew began to read it over. "I've got to commend you guys, you thought of everything. My family thinks I am on vacation and unreachable. My boss thinks I am sick. My superintendent fed my cat since he thinks I'll be out of town for a week on a last-minute call to work. Only the government has the truth, so they shut down part of the park due to a 'rogue bear.' How do we keep this all straight?"

Smiling smugly, Jerry said, "Simple, despite your cell phone working as of—" and paused for a dramatic flash from his smart watch, which didn't happen. Looking a bit defeated, he resumed saying, "When it's working, we'll disable it so unless you answer a call or e-mail, it doesn't read as connected."

"Which fits several of the storylines, and the super?"

"About fifteen minutes before we get to your building, the super will have been pulled away on an emergency."

"You guys are good, and given how my neighbours are used to my hours being unusual, they won't question me being there with others, but how do we cover the move and so forth?"

"Don't worry, kid, we've got it all taken care of. We're professionals, after all."

Andrew tried to suppress a yawn as sleep suddenly called to him, only to hear Jerry say, "Kid, catch some sleep, you've had a hell of a rough ride, and it ain't even half over yet."

****

The next thing Andrew knew, he felt Jerry vigorously shaking him. "Wake up, kid, we're here!"

"Huh?" Looking out the window, Andrew saw his apartment building beside them.

"I owe you an apology, kid. I didn't know Elf cigars had that effect on you humans."

Leaving the driver's side of the van and rushing to the other side, Jerry opened the door to help Andrew out. "There you go kid, get some fresh air, you need it. Clear the lungs, clear your mind, and for the love of God, I pray this clears things up before your wife finds out what happened."

Staggering on his feet, Andrew asked, "What happened?" Despite the cold night air, he still wanted to sleep.

"Know that cigar I was smoking?"

"Yeah, found it weird it didn't smell."

Andrew started to cough, and felt Jerry hit him hard on the back. "There you go, kid, get it all out. Elves call them Dream Cigars—helps you unwind, relax, and pass the time. Thing is, it put you out like a light for eight hours."

Rubbing his temples, Andrew said, "Is that why it's night outside, and I feel like elephants held a tap dancing contest on the top of my head?"

"Yup," Jerry said as he threw Andrew a small, black box. "Put this on, standard issue." Hanging the box off his improvised toga, Andrew watched as pants and a shirt suddenly appeared on him, and Jerry went from a short gnome to someone who could pass as human. As he became more awake, he realized there were two women waiting on the side of the van. He assumed they were Sherry and Bloom. "Holo-disguises. Power supply is limited, which is why we don't use them to mix with you humans," Jerry said in way of explanation before yelling to his sisters, "Yo! Let's go to work, ladies!"

The one with the light green hair put her hands on her hips and leaned forward as she said in disgust, "There is no reason to yell, big bother. We're right here, and it's the middle of the night."

The one with the black hair muttered in agreement, "Yeah. Besides, we're not the one who drugged the human."

"Yeesh, and odds are you two will nag me about that mistake for the next twenty years, right?" Jerry muttered.

Both sisters took several devices from the van before closing it up. Given how late it was, no one noticed their entry into the building, or Andrew's apartment, where a tabby cat charged them. Petting the cat, Andrew said reassuringly, "Don't worry, Charger, these are friends. Strange, but new friends." With that, the cat flipped onto his back as a way of demanding belly pets from the gnomes, with Bloom being the only one ready to do so. Excusing himself, Andrew left the gnomes briefly to change into some normal clothing. Once done and feeling closer to normal, he returned to his living room. "So, how do we move all my stuff, with just the four of us, in the middle of the night without waking anyone up?"

Jerry had turned off his holo-disguise and taken a seat on the sofa with his feet up on the coffee table. "Simple teleporters. We mark down everything which gets relayed to a central device, which then gets moved from there to your new home."

Sarcasm filled Andrew's voice as he said, "And how will Erica react when at, say, two a.m. my video game collection appears in the kitchen unannounced?"

"Gnome and Dwarf construction crews will take measurements of your stuff as it's being teleported, and modify your new home accordingly. It might take a few days to get it all there and set up, but the job will be done."

"So, wait, at two a.m. when Erica is dead asleep, your people are going to undertake major renovations at her place?"

Smiling smugly, Jerry responded, "Go log onto Skype. We'll talk after that."

Walking into his office, he could hear Sherry and Bloom going around the apartment. Sitting down in his chair and logging into Skype, he was surprised to see one new person on his friends list. He suspected he knew who it was, which is why he accepted the person's invitation, and requested to video chat.

"Good morning, Andrew," Erica said from the screen.

"Morning, what has you up at this hour?" He could see the worry lines all over her face. She had chosen to wear a purple blouse the same color as her eyes for this call.

"A few things, but the first was being told my husband had been drugged by government employees! The second is the construction crews being here make it next to impossible to sleep, and I only got in about an hour ago."

"Did I tell you how beautiful that blouse looks on you?"

"No, but thank you for the compliment, and trying to take my mind off of things." Looking him straight in the eye, she said, "I knew what to expect when we got married. I am more worried about you, and how are you taking it."

"Erica, this is just another day at the office for me."

"It shouldn't be. You're human, and a millennial."

Smiling, he replied, "We'll swap stories later, honey. I am tougher than I look."

A big, burly dwarf suddenly appeared on the screen. "Excuse me, miss, we need to shut off the power if we're going to start rewiring the house."

Waving meekly to the screen, Andrew said, "See you soon."

Even though he couldn't see her, he heard her reply, "You will," just as the connection died.

Turning around in his chair, he was not surprised to see Jerry leaning against the door frame. "All right, kid, we need to talk. Now. Part of the gig we got with you."

At which point, Bloom came into the room. "Actually, Gerald, if it's all the same to you, I'll do it."

Raising his voice, he said, "But I am the driver, I'll do it per the contract."

Bloom looked him straight in the eye. "I'll do it. I am just as qualified as you! Think of it as my way of apologizing for trying to grab Andrew's ass—I am here to work, not make a pass at a man." It had been ages since Bloom had felt this level of attraction to anyone.

"All right, I give. I'll go help Sherry mark stuff down for teleport."

Getting up from the chair, Andrew looked down at Bloom. "Where do you want to talk?"

"The kitchen will do fine."

Following her into the kitchen, he watched as she grabbed a soda from his fridge with relative ease. "You want one?"

"Sure."

Sitting down across from him at the four-person table, she said, "By now you've figured out services like this aren't cheap, right?"

"Naturally."

Taking a sip from her soda, she said, "This is more of a bribe by the High Council to you, since they want something from you, something big."

"And that is?" He made a bit of an impatient rolling motion with his hand.

Looking up at him, she said, "We want you to be our new Ambassador to the human world, to help prevent a war that could end all sentient life on this planet." With a quick bit of reflection, she added, "Depending on which side of the High Council you sit on does or does not want the war."

Andrew got a familiar feeling as his jaw started to fall, before he said in protest, "But I am not qualified in the least to be one! Heck, I usually organize people, and fix machines for a living, not talk to people."

Looking at him sympathetically, she said, "You might not be qualified now, but with some help from your clan and a little luck, you have a chance to make it better for all of us."

Taking a sip from his own soda, Andrew replied, "Why me?"

"Since you are human, you grew up in this culture, this environment, and, I hate to say it, you're white. While we know some humans aren't racist, some are, and if we are going to get the treaty changed, we need every edge we can get."

"Maybe you can explain who the High Council is, and then we can work from there?"

"There are countless non-human sentient races on Earth. Some evolved on this planet, some arrived here from the stars as refugees. The High Council is comprised of the three strongest military races, and the three with the largest populations, and with one random seat to one of the smaller populations. That random seat acts as a moderator."

"Okay..."

"Some factions on either side want to go to all-out war with the humans, and we know some have already been bending the treaty."

"Bending it how?"

"Know flight 370 from Malaysia? Or how about Indian Air Force AN-32? Maybe even Pakistan international Airlines flight 404?"

"Hey, flight 404 went missing in '89, close to thirty years ago."

"When a race has an expected life span of two thousand years, thirty years is but the blink of an eye."

"What about them?"

"Certain members of the Lower Council suspect dragons on the High Council are attacking aircrafts they believe can be made to disappear. Some golems are causing earthquakes, and you get the idea."

"So, missing airplanes and natural disasters are them bending the treaty?"

"Think of them like raids. There is no response by the other side, so they'll up the attacks, until—"

"War," Andrew finished for her.

"Now you get it."

Fooling around with his half-empty soda can, Andrew said, "This is heavy. Can you please inform the council on my behalf that I'd like a few days to think this over, talk it out with Erica, maybe ask a few questions?"

Smiling measuredly at him, she replied, "I think that is more than reasonable."

Jerry stuck his head into the kitchen. "Yo, you two. Everything is marked, your new place is ready, it's time to teleport!"

Getting up from her chair, Bloom said, "I was thinking about driving back to Andrew's new home with him. That way I can get to know him a bit—" She cut herself off, changing tack and saying, "I can brief him more on our people, and our ways. Assuming he agrees."

Like everyone else present, Andrew had heard her slip, and said, "It makes sense to me to more fully understand your people, and the role they want me to play in your society."

"All right, but remember, it's an eight-hour drive out there since you two lack the special license to go through stuff," Jerry says, before throwing the van keys to Bloom, giving her a funny look as he did so.

In an instant, everything in the apartment vanished. Andrew had meant to ask if could move his computer the old-fashioned way. "Come on," said Bloom, leading the way out. "Maybe we'll take shifts as we drive."

Chapter 4

The drive back to Erica's home was taking them longer than what Jerry had said since they had stopped to eat and do some shopping. Andrew had discovered that, like other non-human species, Gnomes could eat human food, but had to watch out for certain ingredients. Several times he had offered to pay for food, but Bloom swore that the council would pay for it, and had taken all the receipts.

Stopping at an open park so they could rest, Andrew saw Bloom was on the verge of tears as they approached a picnic table with some food. "Bloom, did I say something wrong in the van?"

"No, it's not that, it's all the death we're seeing." She paused to catch her breath. "It's getting to me."

"What do you mean? We haven't seen one dead body."

Sitting down at the table, her eyes rimmed with red, she said, "Are you blind? How many dead animals have we seen out there along the road?" She swept an arm out to indicate where the highway was.

"I don't know. A few, I figure."

Starting to cry now, she replied, "We've seen twenty-five of them." Now bursting into full-blown tears, she continued, "Twenty-five of them that have been killed by impact with a vehicle, most likely driven by a human."

"Well, it's been like that since humans started to get around on machines over animals."

Andrew saw Bloom's green eyes puff up as she kept crying. "It doesn't make it right," she said, trying to hold back her tears now.

Reaching across the table, Andrew patted her on the shoulder. "You are right."

Smiling a bit, she sniffled back her tears, saying, "You mean that, don't you?"

"Yes."

"Even my brother doesn't say that, and he knows about my affinity."

"Your affinity?"

As Bloom got up from the table, Andrew couldn't help but notice that she could pass as human. She was a little over four-foot-two, and even with her green hair and green dress, she wouldn't be the first person to fall in love with a colour.

Walking on the grass, she asked, "Why do you think I wear so much green?"

"Because it matches your hair?"

"No," she replies, laughing lightly at his compliment. Crouching down to the ground, she rested a hand, almost in reverence, just above the grass. "It's because while most gnomes love machines and understand them, I am a bit of a hybrid; I understand machines, and also nature."

"Is that why when you teleported stuff out of my apartment, you handled Charger and my plants?"

Smiling, she said, "Yes." Every part of her wanted to rush to him and hug him. "You understand, don't you?"

"I don't understand, but I can respect we all have our own gifts, and should have the right to use them as long as no harm comes to others. Or, if you must harm others, to use it only to defend others from greater harm."

"That's what I love about you humans," Bloom said. "You are so mentally flexible, is it no wonder the High Council wants one to talk to the others."

Blushing a bit, Andrew said, "You want me to take the job, don't you?"

"Yup. Let's finish up lunch and get back on the road."

"All right."

****

While they spoke a lot during the rest of the drive back, Bloom kept mentally going back to their conversation in the park, and several observations she had made about Andrew at his apartment. She hadn't told him the depth of her affinity for animals and life. It let her communicate with Charger, who had told her how good a human Andrew was. Unknown to him, she had decided on doing something she hadn't tried in over twenty-five years based on their limited time together.

She saw the surprise on Andrew's face as they pulled into the freshly dug tunnel connecting Erica's garage to the main road; she told him it was normal for them to build tunnels like this quickly. Lights tied into sensors turned on and off as the van made its trip to the main bay where Andrew saw his car parked. Getting out of the van, he started to look it over. "Maybe I was too hard on Hotwire for what she did. My car looks great." Going over it in several spots, he continued, "She even redid the paint and body work."

Closing the van door behind her, Bloom now stood outside of it and said, "Andrew, mind waiting here for a few moments? I need to speak with Erica, government stuff."

"All right," he said, opening his car up. "I want to check out what Hotwire did to my car and cell anyways."

"Thanks."

Before getting onto the lift that would ascend with her to the surface level, Bloom took a stick of green lipstick from her purse and applied it. It was part of steeling herself, like her father had taught her over fifty years ago.

Despite being a gnome by birth, she was very much the daughter of a dwarf king, and since she was from a second wife, she was no princess. She was still, however, a warrior, and warriors fought for what they wanted. In Andrew, she saw a man she wanted in her life as a mate, and the potential father of her children.

Walking up to the door of the house, few people who knew Bloom would recognize her now as each step was taken with precision. Everything associated with gnomes in her body language vanished the second she made up her mind about what she had to do. Knocking on the door, Erica opened it and looked down at her. "You are?"

Dropping to one knee, Bloom said, "I am Bloom, late of Clan Chronoton, daughter of the Dwarf King Malor, ruler of all dwarves that reside in the human lands known as Norway and Sweden. Long may he reign." Looking up at Erica, she asked, "You are Erica, member of Herd Swifthoof, First Lady and wife to Andrew of the Humans? It is to my understanding that he has no second wives lined up?"

"You are informed correctly, Bloom. Yes, I am Erica, Andrew's First Wife and lady. Would you come in?"

"Thank you, my lady." Getting up, Bloom followed Erica into the house. She asked, "You respect the conventions of our people, where we respect each other's traditions?"

"Without question, but my Husband and Lord and I have spoken of allowing human flexibilities within our clan. Is that acceptable to you?"

Walking into the living room, Erica sat down in a corner while Bloom stood ram-rod straight in the middle of it, facing her. "It is. May I state my business with you, my lady?"

"Naturally."

"Despite failing to earn the right to be a First Wife and Lady like you when your mother was just a filly, even now I would redo those tests, and fight to prove I could be his first wife. However, that would dishonor your own accomplishments, something I will not do."

Erica found it weird to hear a woman who appeared to be a gnome speaking like a dwarf, with a rough, almost abrasive tone to her voice. Generally, gnomes were known for being cheerful and friendly. Smiling, she said, "Thank you. You honour us. What would you have of him and us, Bloom?"

Bloom proceeded to unzip the top of her dress. With almost military precision, she undid her bra, and let Erica see her large breasts that, coupled with her affinity, had long caused countless gnome men to not see her as a worthy mate. Gnome men preferred women with smaller breasts. The house was air conditioned, so her pink nipples immediately stuck out. The bra was a normal cloth one with a simple underwire. Like the rest of her clothing, it was green. She laid it on the floor.

Reaching down now under her dress, she felt for the hemline of her green and white striped panties. Pulling them down, Bloom felt relief as fresh, cold air greeted her vagina—her panties had been soaked for hours. The only thing better than cold air would be Andrew's hard cock, but that would be for later, assuming things went well. Walking up to Erica, she said, "Please feel these, my lady." She handed over her panties to Erica.

Confused, Erica said, "These are soaking wet."

"And not of urine, I assure you. I would not dishonour you or him in that way." Taking them back, Bloom placed them in one cup of her bra. From her purse that was on the floor, she pulled out a small data card, holding it up for Erica to see. "My dowry," she said, "and biographical information."

Placing the card on the panties, she closed one bra cup over the other. Bloom then kissed it firmly to ensure her green lipstick stuck to it and was clearly visible. She then marched up to Erica and presented the package to her while bowing on one knee. Getting up, she clicked her heels as she marched back to the middle of the room to stand at attention, waiting for Erica to say something.

"You realize there are other candidates that have made themselves known to us, correct, Bloom?"

"Of course, human men rarely join our people."

"And how did you come to know of my husband?"

"I was part of the team assigned to help teleport his home into yours, and convey the will of the High Council to him. On the drive back, I got to know him, and he believes we are now speaking of government matters." In a sense, they were, given how tightly family was connected to government. As one politician once said, politics start at the family dinner table.

"At least you know him better than the other candidates. I cannot guarantee you a chance at the role of second wife on his side, but I will make sure he knows of your interest."

"That is all I ask, my lady."

"I assure you, he and I will speak of this in the next few days, and I will explain to him the meaning of your application."

"Thank you, my lady."

"If I might ask you one favor and give you some advice?"

"Certainly."

Erica tried to suppress a smile from forming on her lips, but it still reached her eyes as she said, "You might want to pull up your dress before you tell Andrew we're done here."

"Oh, right," Bloom said as she pulled it up. Knowing she was dismissed, she left Erica's presence. Descending down the lift, she saw Andrew waiting.

"How did it go with Erica?" he asked.

"Better than expected, everything was settled." Walking back towards the van, she heard Andrew further ask, "Will I see you around?"

Opening and closing the van's door, she called out from the open driver's side window, "We'll see." The ball was in their court now, even if Andrew didn't know it. For the first time in ages, Bloom thought she saw a Clan she could contribute to that had space for her, with a male head that could provide her with the children she wanted to bear.

Driving home was uneventful for Bloom. Pulling into Gnome Express garage, she saw Jerry on the catwalk waiting for her. Exiting the van, he called out to her from above, "You did it, didn't you?"

Putting her hands on her hips, she asked, "Do what?"

"You—you left your stuff behind." Jerry had never been comfortable with female dwarf mating rituals.

"Even if I did, *Gerald*," she said, making his name sound unpleasant, "it's none of your business."

His feet clanked on the metal stairs as he ran down to the van. "It is my business, missy, since I am the one who patched you up last time, and I don't want to see you hurt again." Bloom had lost count of how many times over the years he had torn her down "for her own good."

Bloom started to walk away, but Jerry caught up with her, grabbing her by the arm to turn her around. "I mean it, Bloom, I care about you. Last time you did your thing and the clan rejected you, you went into a dark hole for a decade. Darker than Sherry."

With steel in her voice, Bloom responded, "Yes, Gerald, I remember it." Shaking his hand off her arm, she continued, "Now, let me go, it's been a long day, and I want to shower and sleep."

Watching her walk away, Jerry called out to her, "I mean it, sis, I only have the best of intentions for you."

******

After the last few days of things being far from normal, Andrew was glad to have a morning that was close to normal for a change. Waking up, he felt Charger purring up a storm behind him, as was his cat's custom. Erica held one of his hands, and, stretching herself forward for a moment, she kissed him, murmuring, "Morning, sleepyhead. Time to wake up."

"What a beautiful sight to wake up to," he said.

"You say that to just me, or all the Centaurian women you know?"

"Just you."

"Smart man."

When the dwarves and gnomes had expanded Erica's house, they had more than tripled the size of her bedroom to accommodate Andrew's bed, night stand, and dresser. Getting up, Andrew picked his t-shirt up off the floor. He picked up Erica's too, throwing it to her.

"You know, we don't have to put tops on—it's just us here," she said.

"Yeah, but how else will we know we want to have fun?" Andrew replied. Getting close to her, he playfully reached under one of her breasts to lift it, and she saw his penis becoming hard under his PJs. "True," she said. Making a grab for it, he warned her, "You start it, you finish it."

"Always," she said, smiling, reaching down to release him from the confines of his PJs. With them on the floor, she reached down for his penis. She heard him wince in pain as she wrapped one of her hands around it, and, as if not to break the mood, he whispered, "Gentle." Clearly, she had done it a bit too tightly.

Easing her grip a bit she started to play with it as she had seen from videos online. She could feel it growing in her hand, and he started to pant the more she did it. Using one his hands he reached under her shirt to play with one of her breasts, as a thumb kept playing with one of her nipples. The pleasure he was giving her almost caused her to lose control and grip his cock too tightly. However, at the last moment before he knew it would happen she stopped herself from doing it.

Locked in a cycle of pleasure, Andrew used his free hand to guide hers, "Here," he said. "Play with the head, its like when I played with your clit."

Understanding what he meant, while running a hand up and down his shaft she used her thumb to play with the head of his cock. Just from his reaction she knew she was going a good job. It was getting harder for them to focus on what they were doing, until given how she was handling Andrew's cock she felt his semen flow out before she saw it, and it left a mess on the floor.

Both of them seemed to feel more relaxed after what they just did to each other. She knew if she was human Andrew would've played with her woman hood as she had played with his cock. It was one of those problems when different species became involved with one another. She pulled back, smiling, feeling a bit of the glow she had come to associate with how she felt after sex. "Feeling better?" she asked.

"After a hand job like that, yes. Thank you," he replied, kissing her passionately to show his gratitude.

In a sense, their morning routines hadn't changed for either of them; both went to their respective coffee machines. Andrew made his instant pancakes, which made Erica question how he could eat so much sugar in the morning, while he asked her how she could eat such a bland breakfast of just muffins. Both of them read their tablets as they ate breakfast. Andrew offered to wash their dishes. Erica was still sitting at the table as he worked. She said, "It's Saturday, so I know we have the day off, and there is something we need to talk about."

"I know, the action figure collection needs to be downsized or removed, right?"

"No. Actually I am fine as long as they remain in your office." Pausing for a moment, she continued, "There is something in the fridge for us, and its value needs to be explained to you. It's in the dark Tupperware container."

Putting the dishes on the rack to dry, he pulled the plug to let the water drain out of the sink. Only then did he head over to the fridge, pulling out the Tupperware container that Erica had mentioned. Bringing it to the table where she was still sitting, she opened it up, while Andrew sat down across from her. Within it was Bloom's bra, just as it was last night, as were its contents.

Pulling it out, Erica began to explain. "By closing her bra and kissing it, it shows our female caller has sealed her offer to us."

"Her offer?"

"It's what's within the bra." Erica opened up the green bra and held up the data card. "This is her dowry, and biography. We can use my tablet to read its contents."

"So we can know more about her?"

"Precisely."

"And those aren't what I think they are, are they?" Andrew asked, pointing to a pair of still-wet panties that Bloom had left in one of her cups.

"Yes, they are," said Erica. "It's to show you how attracted she is to you, and as for the bra, it's to show you how well she can nurse any children she has with you. What we have here is part of an old dwarf tradition, mixed with some modern tech when they really want someone."

Andrew thought for a moment. "Hmm... Who made this offering?"

"Bloom. She was part of your transportation orientation team yesterday."

Chuckling, Andrew told Erica how Bloom tried to grab his ass when they'd first met. "With that in mind, honey, what do you think? This is your world."

"I say we meet her. Others have expressed interest in marrying into our clan, but nothing so personal or affectionate."

"Consider it done then." Getting up from the table, Andrew told Erica he was going for a quick ride on his bike, and asked that she set up the meeting later that afternoon with Bloom.

****

At that moment, neither Andrew nor Erica would've recognized Bloom given how she was now dressed. Gone were the frilly dress, the pig tails, the air of cuteness that gnomes were known for having. Instead, she was a hardened gnome preparing for battle, even if it was just training. She was clad in leather pants that hugged her ass, and a leather jacket as tight as a second skin. Her green hair was tied up in a bun, and she was marching towards a room in Gnome Express dedicated solely to holograms, so she could train. She wore a snarl on her lips that in some ways didn't come naturally to her, but she wore it to help her mindset.

Entering the room, she pulled her shortsword out from its sheath that hung on her hip. She then closed her eyes, and calmed her mind. *Ride the rage like a surfer does the top of a wave*, her papa used to tell her. In an instant, she was hyper attuned to the world—nothing was beyond her sight and mind. Throwing her sword, she narrowly missed Jerry who had entered the room. He jumped out of the way to avoid it, and, from the ground, he said, "You trying to kill me?"

Knowing her place, she said apologetically, "No, Jerry, it was an accident. I am sorry." She walked over to the wall where her sword was a good three inches in, and started to pull it out. "What do you want? We don't have a job until this afternoon, and I want to get some training in."

Holding up a phone, he said, "Call for you. Someone named Erica?"

Stopping her efforts to pull the sword from the wall, she grabbed the phone from Jerry's hand, and, in an instant, he watched as his sister went from what he coined "Gnome Warrior" to her normal, cheery self. After several moments of conversation with the person on the other end, she returned the phone to him. Looking at the clock on the wall, she said, "All right, I have a few hours to train, then you, Hotwire, and Sherry have the move. I have something very important to do, so I am skipping it."

He got up and dusted himself off. "We have the Werewolf move this afternoon, and they have several biologicals. What are we supposed to do if you aren't there?" Glaring at her, he added, "Moving those things is your job!"

A little bit of courage broke through her heart as she said, "I will do it next time, Jerry." Bracing her foot against the wall, she gave her sword a good, solid pull. "Use a few drones and the van. For the animals, use stasis collars or ask the owners for a hand!"

"Bloom, remember your place! In this company, moving biologicals is your job!"

Pulling the sword out from the wall, she gave it a once-over for any damage. "I have a more pressing appointment this afternoon now."

"And what could be more important than a move?"

Trying to calm herself, she stretched her sword arm out. "Remember how yesterday I 'did my thing,' as you put it?"

"Yeah, what about it?"

"Erica is the first lady and wife, and they've invited me over to talk this afternoon."

Using the wisdom he had picked up over the years of abusing and molding his sisters, Jerry knew when to strike. Right now was far from the perfect time; if he did, Bloom would put him through a steel I-beam, head first. Later, when the time was right, he'd punish her for this.

****

Bloom never told her brother or sisters, but practising swordplay was one of the ways she burned off her needs. All non-human races tried to practise the idea of not having sex outside of marriage, even if you weren't a First Wife or a Husband. In the end, there was only so much you could do to yourself.

That might be changing for her soon, she thought. She had always been attracted to non-traditional gnome mates. While Sherry might swoon over the occasional vampire, or Hotwire go gaga for a new piece of tech, she found she preferred races taller than her own. She also knew how rare it was for species so much taller than her to see her as a viable mate.

Maybe it was like that old song she heard when she was little—when you wish on a star, and if your heart is true, you will get your heart's desire. Maybe that was why she had applied to so few Clans over the years; perhaps somewhere the hands of fate were going to give her what she wanted most if she just waited long enough.

Driving towards Erica's home in her small car, she couldn't help but reflect back on her life. Back in Europe, they'd had it all. With father securely on the throne, even someone not in the line of succession had it all. She needed teachers, she had them; she wanted potential mates, they lined up around the block three people deep. Then Jerry made the mistake that sent them into exile in North America of all places. Their poor mother had died of a broken heart and drinking, shortly after they had originally arrived in Brooklyn. The four of them had spent the last fifty years struggling to build up Gnome Express so they could at least live independently. Living in a warehouse was so hard on Bloom, given all the concrete and lack of plants.

Turning off the road, she descended down the ramp and into a tunnel that had been dug towards Erica's home. The garage door opened as it scanned her car, and knew she was expected. She knew what the government had been willing to pay for, and what Erica had paid for the upgrade of this tunnel. She knew if she married into this family, she'd be expected to work, and nothing could get her back into the life of luxury she had known as a child. However, if they accepted her into their clan, then at least she'd be near plants and animals again.

She'd also be free of Jerry. For a brief moment, her warrior heart shuddered at the countless indignities he had made her suffer over the years.

Pulling her tan car to a stop next to Andrew's, she hopped out and looked at herself in the mirror one last time. She wanted everything to be perfect. She had chosen to do her hair in one ponytail, and her gold necklace and earrings were small, but stylish. She was wearing green pants today that matched her hair. The white blouse she had chosen was tighter than the top of the dress she wore yesterday. She wanted to emphasize she had the goods, so to speak. She had heard human men were attracted to women with larger busts. While she knew she couldn't compete with Erica in that regard—few non-humans could compete with a Centaur—it didn't mean she couldn't flaunt what she had. Walking on the cement floor up to the lift, she was glad she didn't do anything stupid like wear heels for this meeting, date, interview... *What do you call this?* she wondered as the lift took her up to the surface.

Walking up to the door, she knocked and waited for Erica to answer. After greeting each other, Bloom asked, "Where is Andrew? It was supposed to be the three of us, am I correct, my lady?"

Stepping outside, Erica said, "Andrew has been unexpectedly delayed by another matter, and he'll be joining us later." *I hope,* thought Erica. She had called his cell several times since he went cycling and he had not answered.

Stepping out of the house and down the stairs from the stoop, Erica lowered herself. "If it's not too much to ask, would you mind mounting me?"

Bloom's jaw almost went slack. "Excuse me? Isn't that for members of your clan only, Lady Erica?"

Bringing her hand up to her throat in the style of old royalty, Erica responded, "My husband and I have already decided to drop the honorific of my Lord or my Lady unless it's a formal situation. Please just address me as Erica." Her tail rose up playfully. "While it is true my people consider mounting us as an intimate act, given your...presentation, I won't complain if you don't."

Mounting Erica as instructed, Bloom asked her, "Is that one of Andrew's t-shirts?"

Pulling down on the black garment to try and cover her exposed midriff, Erica replied, "Yup, he seems to have dozens of them. I doubt he'll mind my borrowing one, even if it is a bit tight up front." Raising off the ground, Erica began to trot them away. "I love him, but clothes shopping is on the to-do list with him."

"Agreed. Mind you, it could be worse. He could dress like Jerry."

"Jerry?"

Bloom went into a prolonged explanation about how Jerry, her brother, kept buying clothes everyone felt made their eyes burn out with all their different colours. The forest around them encouraged her to cut her usual speech short. "If I may, Erica, where are we going?"

"Do you remember your data file saying you have an affinity with plants and animals?"

"Yes."

"Think of what I am about to show you as a test of that skill."

Erica could feel the strength in Bloom's legs and arms as she grabbed the Centaur. "Then let's ride!" It surprised Erica to feel such strength in the little gnome, but then again, Bloom was taller than the average gnome. Most likely something to do with having a dwarf father. Going as fast as she could, Erica was surprised when Bloom asked her a question. "I'm wondering... How many candidates are there for the role of second wife?"

Focusing on where she was going, Erica responded, "I am sorry, Andrew and I agreed to not tell anyone that fact, but I can tell you that you are the first person we're seeing about filling his side of the wives."

With that news, Bloom broke into a grin, even if Erica couldn't see it. After all the setbacks in her life, maybe now she had a chance to live a life she wanted. She was surprised when Erica slowed down and said, "We're here," as they entered a clearing. Dropping down, Erica let Bloom off her back and explained, "This is one of my failures, Bloom, and I am hoping you can help me with it."

With Bloom's back to her, Erica threw Andrew's cotton t-shirt off of her; it felt good to be free of its confinement. Feeling the sun on her breasts always felt great to her—it was one of the reasons she had bought so much land, so she could walk around nude and no one would care. Walking through the grass, Bloom said, "What's the problem here?"

"The problem is that I wanted to grow wild grains here, but they never took."

Still not knowing that Erica had disrobed behind her, Bloom nodded. "Yeah, I know the feeling." She thought back to the last time she had eaten a nice, fat wild rabbit she had shot through, eye to eye, with an arrow. She appreciated the taste of wild food, that blend of not too fat, not too lean meat. Bending down, the gnome picked up some soil, feeling it. "You have the right soil here, it's just a matter of—EEEK!" Turning around, she saw Erica's breasts. Covering up her eyes, she stammered out, "Why—why—why are you exposed like that?"

Walking towards Bloom, Erica said playfully, "Since it feels good to feel the sun on my breasts, and not to be confined by clothing." Shaking her head, she continued, "Besides, I figured if I showed you mine, you'd show me yours."

Trying to cover her eyes from the approaching Centaur, Bloom asked, "You want to see my breasts?"

"No, I want to see all of you!" Erica declared, her arms stretched out wide as she walked around Bloom. "Look around us—we're in the middle of a fallow field in the height of summer, and clothes can be so confining sometimes."

Bowing down so she could reach Bloom's ear, Erica whispered, "Besides, what belongs to the husband, belongs to the wife, and vice versa."

Still stammering with her hands over her eyes, Bloom replied, "Your—your—your point?"

Sitting down so she was right across from Bloom, Erica reached out to the terrified gnome as gently as she could and rested an arm on her shoulder. "Bloom, I didn't mean to scare you. I meant to test you, and possibly seduce you."

Keeping her eyes closed, Bloom asked, "Test me how?"

Shaking her head, despite knowing Bloom couldn't see it, Erica replied, "I know some species have a problem with casual nudity. I wanted to know your reaction to it."

"Did Andrew undergo the same test?" Bloom's voice squeaked.

"No, but he did undergo a different one, with different stakes."

Slowly opening her eyes, Bloom was confronted with the largest pair of breasts she had ever seen in person. "I understand. Hey, you have no tan lines!"

Showing off a bit, Erica put her hands behind her head as she turned left to right to give Bloom an unobscured view of them. "Yes, one of the advantages of owning so much land. You can tan like this and no one will complain."

Looking down at her own blouse, Bloom asked, "May I?"

"Certainly."

With care, Bloom worked the buttons of her white blouse from top to bottom, removing it and hanging it off some tall grass. Erica took in a deep gasp of air as she saw more of Bloom's skin. "How did you get all those bruises, scars, and cuts?"

Looking at several of them, Bloom replied, "Moving accidents. You know how it is, right?"

"No. Does Gnome Express have many employees?"

Getting down once again to examine the soil, Bloom replied, "More of a family business—just my brother, sisters and

I." Feeling the soil between her fingers, she said, "I have good news, and bad news."

Erica laughed at that statement; life rarely seemed pure. "What's the bad news?"

"You need fertilizer and water here. Given how I suspect you want real wild grains, you'll need to attract the correct critters to drop it here, while not clearing the field."

Walking forward, Erica asked Bloom to follow her. "The water problem can be solved," she said, stepping though some of the grass and revealing a small pond. Stepping into the pond, Erica asked Bloom to join her with a wave of her hand. Reluctantly, the gnome took off her shoes, and then her pants. Commenting on it, Erica said, "I can see you've gone commando."

"Yeah." Bloom didn't want to tell Erica how poor she was, that by giving away a pair of her panties, she was down to only two pairs. Looking down at her vagina, she said, "I hope Andrew likes the landing strip effect."

Chuckling, Erica brought her hand up to her mouth. "I am sure he'll like how the carpet matches the drapes."

Looking Erica in the eyes, Bloom said, "Thank you, Erica. For all this."

"For what?" Erica asked, following Bloom as she walked around the edge of pond.

"For making me feel free enough to walk around here naked, given how much...joy I get from it. It's hard to describe how I feel." Stopping for a moment, Bloom just wiggled her toes in the warm soil. "You know, maybe one day I can get a more uniform tan and look as pretty as you," Bloom said, turning away a bit from Erica as she complimented her, hoping to hide her blushing face.

"Who says you aren't?"

Looking down at her feet, Bloom replied, "It doesn't matter."

"You know what they say—attack one member of a clan, you attack them all."

"I know." Bloom's voice was filled with dejection.

"Bloom, could you turn around and face me, please?"

As Bloom turned around, part of Erica was concerned that the damage to her body wasn't attributed only to simple "moving accidents." "Bloom, do you think Andrew or I would be interested in getting to know you better if we found you unattractive?"

The gnome, still refusing to look up, said, "No."

"Despite what humans say—never judge a book by its cover—a cover does attract the reader."

"True."

Urging Bloom with her voice, Erica said, "Please, Bloom, look up at me." As Bloom looked up into Erica's eyes, Erica continued, "You have nothing to be ashamed of in your looks."

Erica was surprised when Bloom walked over and hugged her. It was the kind of hug that spoke volumes about the amount of pain Bloom had endured. Despite being aware of how large their respective breasts were, it wasn't until they were in close contact that Erica realized this fact. In some part of her mind, she couldn't help but wonder if they were the same cup size, but this was all put aside as she heard Bloom crying, thanking her repeatedly.

Stroking the gnome's green hair, she replied, "Whatever for?"

With her head half buried into Erica's neck, Bloom said, "Because of my gift, the land and animals tell me things. They told me you are a good person, and it's true."

"I didn't realize the extent of your affinity for this kind of thing."

Sniffling as she tried to hold back tears of joy, Bloom said, "Looks weird if I put in the data card that I can communicate with plants and animals."

"True. Now why in heaven's name do you think you're ugly?"

Bloom stepped away from Erica. "It's not just the uneven tan, it's these," she said, indicating her large breasts. "Gnome men find them ugly, and, when combined with my gift and my tastes, it's been hard for me to find someone special in my life who will accept me. I mean, even when I go clothes shopping, I have been told in gnome stores to go to another species' store due to them."

Looking at her big, white breasts, the dash of wind caused her nipples to stand out. "One man even told me I should have reduction surgery if I wanted to join his clan because of the kind of freak I am." Holding up her breasts, it was like she was reliving the rejection. "But I won't!"

Putting a firm hand on Bloom's shoulder, Erica said, "And you don't! Not in this clan!"

"Does that mean...?" she asked hopefully.

Smiling, Erica said, "Yes, Bloom, I won't veto you. Now it's up to Andrew, and he does understand the power of the gift you gave us." *As do I,* she thought, *it's just a matter of him understanding the other situation.*

Launching herself at Erica, Bloom hugged her so hard that Erica thought she'd break as the gnome wrapped her arms and legs around her. Where before it felt like Bloom was facing some inner turmoil and she needed physical reassurance that everything would be all right, this time it was just sheer joy that drove the gnome.

Breast to breast, it took some work on Bloom's part, but she managed to get her lips lined up with Erica's. Kissing the Centaur passionately, it was she who needed this, to feel reaffirmation that Erica had spoken the truth. She began to rub her vagina along the Centaur's taut human belly. Given their height difference, she was rubbing the lower part of the Centaur's breasts with the top of her pubic hair when she went up.

Erica had never been with a humanoid woman before, and was caught completely flat-hooved to Bloom launching herself at her like this. She had gone from leading to following. She could feel the heat building in Bloom's vagina the more the gnome rubbed it against her; every time Erica tried to drift a hand downwards to play with it, the gnome whispered "no" between kisses or pushed her hand away.

Bloom didn't know how much longer she could hold out; every time her vagina went up and down Erica's belly, it felt like she was going to explode. It felt so good!

Thanks to Andrew, Erica wasn't as sex-crazed as Bloom was, but she was thankful she was in the pond since she could feel herself warming up. Bending forward, she pushed the gnome onto the earth. She heard Bloom plead with her between gasps of pleasure, "Please don't take me."

Erica knew that the gnome didn't want her to attempt to penetrate her. "I won't," she said reassuringly.

"Thank you," Bloom gasped out. Releasing herself from Erica, she lay on the ground, fully exposed to the Centaur. "Please take care of me." Without really trying, Erica saw how excited Bloom was about her, as she was about Andrew when he had ridden her yesterday.

Looking up at the gnome from this angle was very unusual, as she could just see Bloom's face over her breasts. Running a few fingers casually over the gnome's outer lips, she could feel Bloom shake in pleasure, her toes curling. Lowering herself downward, Erica brushed her hair out of her eyes as she began to kiss the clitoris hood, and worked her way onto the clitoris itself. Kissing it, sucking on it, even sometimes running her tongue around it like a lollipop—all of which seemed to drive the gnome wild with ecstasy. She didn't know how long Bloom held out until she orgasmed, spraying Erica's face with fluid. Sounding exhausted, she heard the gnome once again whisper, "Thank you."

Getting out of the water, Erica lay beside the gnome, who grabbed her hand and learned over to clean her face with her tongue. Erica laughed a bit as the gnome tickled her nose with her tongue. Seeming to have regained her breath, Bloom said, "I mean it, thank you for that. When I felt the natural strength here, I needed some way to release myself."

"I understand, Bloom. Just realize one thing, and promise me another."

"That is?" asked the gnome as she wiggled closer to Erica.

"A good marriage is more than good sex, and that once you've recovered a bit, you'll take care of me?"

"I know, but good sex doesn't hurt, does it?" asked the gnome as she lowered herself and started to lick Erica's nipples—a silent answer to the aforementioned promise.

Holding back a moan of pleasure, Erica replied, "No, it doesn't." She stroked Bloom's hair, gasping, "Please keep doing that."

In both women's minds, they wished Andrew was there as they started to learn more about each other, and both of them, in their wildest imaginations, couldn't begin to imagine where he was as they enjoyed themselves and the great outdoors.

****

Andrew woke up with the mother of all headaches, and his clothes were soaking wet. He could smell sulfur in the air around him. The last thing he remembered was he had stopped while cycling to relax by a small pond. It sounded like someone was cracking a whip near him as an annoyed female voice said, "Wake up, you miserable homo sapien! Wake up! Even royalty can't get away with murder in circumstances like this!"

Feeling out his surroundings, Andrew realized he was on a chair, his hands bound by zip ties. Letting a finger drift down, he found a small, sharp metal shard nearby. He could use that to his advantage, if he needed to escape. For some reason, his host had decided to blindfold him and leave his legs free.

A whooshing noise filled the air, followed by heat, and the scratching of something on cement. He assumed his host was on the same material he was. He heard her say, "If he dies, I don't know who I will kill first. You, girl," the voice snarled, "or those elves I hired to kidnap him in the first place!"

He heard something fly through the air and smash, sounding like wood, before the voice commanded, "Stay in that corner until I tell you to get out of it, you stupid girl! I don't care what you claim your abilities are."

Another female voiced filled the air; it sounded less commanding as it stammered out, "Y-y-yes, Mother."

Though this was his first time being kidnapped, Andrew knew there was only so much information he could gain with his eyes closed. Besides, maybe his hosts would give him an aspirin at the very least to deal with this headache. Opening up his eyes a bit, he said, "I am awake, just hard to open my eyes since I have a massive headache. Don't suppose you have some painkillers on hand?"

Something snapped as the other voice he assumed was his host said, "Get the man some water, and some painkillers. Now!" Andrew felt the wind on his face as his host moved around. *She has to be big*, he thought, but couldn't be sure who it was. While the council hadn't officially offered him the job of Ambassador yet, he had started to do research on them. He wanted to know the job and the people before he accepted it. The voice went on to say, "I do apologize for this, traditions and all. In the old days, it was so much easier for my kind to be out in the open. Now, you pesky humans with your satellites have made it so much harder for my kind and that thrice-damned treaty."

He felt someone grab his head and force it back, as what he assumed was a painkiller was dropped down into his mouth, along with some water. *Must be a servant,* he thought, if he was right about who his host was. Feeling the effects of the drug instantly, he said, "Queen Nataganazar?" doing his best to pronounce her name, the way it said she preferred on her Wiki page. "Is there really a need for these theatrics? I mean, if you wanted to talk with me, surely you could've called me, e-mailed?"

"As I stated, my dear boy, tradition. Back when males led my people, we were known for abducting mortals we wanted to mate with, so when the women took over, we must do as they did." Andrew's host didn't confirm or deny who was holding him hostage.

Bringing his head up and trying to face the sound of her voice, he replied, "Those blinded to tradition forget the power of free will and thought, ma'am. Thus, those bound to tradition face the consequences of reality when tradition no longer serves society, but cripples it."

"True."

"How about taking off the blindfold?"

A clapping filled the air, and, if Andrew didn't know any better, he smelled large quantities of water now in it. The blindfold was removed, and before him stood Queen Nataganazar, undisputed ruler of all dragons on Earth. She was resting on all four of her legs, looking right at him. Her Wiki page hadn't shamed her in any way. Large, dark red scales covered her from end to end, her torso bigger than a pair of M1 Abrams sideways. She was rumoured to be well over five hundred years old. She led the largest military force on the planet, with conservative estimates from her governments' Wiki page saying if the Dragon Empire went on a full assault, even the US military would fall within a week, and that included emptying their nuclear arsenal. Now, here she was before him examining him like a cat would a wounded mouse.

"My thanks, Queen Nataganazar. You mentioned this being a traditional kidnapping?"

"Yes," she said. As she stepped aside, Andrew was able to ascertain that they were in a what appeared to be warehouse, and an empty one at that. He didn't know what dragons normally considered home. "As I said earlier, tradition."

"If this is tradition, then you want to marry me? No offence, but I have a first wife, and you aren't my type."

"None taken. You are a bit young for my tastes. No, in fact I had to do what my daughter lacked the fire to," Queen Nataganazar said, her voice filled with scorn.

Looking around, over half the warehouse was pitch back. Knowing that Queen Nataganazar was known for her temper, Andrew tried to be as respectful as possible when he said, "Your daughter, ma'am? There appears to be no one else here but us."

"Oh, she's there," she snarled. "Show yourself, girl! Don't force me to come into the shadows and drag you out."

The other voice he had heard before spoke, sounding a bit more child-like than before. "I don't wanna."

"Either come out, or I show him everything."

"Show him then, I don't care," the other voice said defiantly.

Speaking to the shadows, Queen Nataganazar said, "Very well then." Turning her head towards Andrew, she said, "Some free advice, good sir, don't have children. Even after two hundred years, that one is still a pain in the scales."

Picking up a remote her body had blocked from Andrew's view, she clicked several buttons and a rather large screen lowered down. This was followed by several photos and videos of he and Erica together intimately, and not just after their first time together. Some of the footage showed both of them after an encounter, and even before by months. Which led to several long-term questions, but the revelations were obvious to him as the blood drained from his face in shock. "The Centaurs would go to war over this in a second! They consider personal privacy one of their highest laws! The second Erica and I wed, I was considered a citizen of their people. Even with non-sexual photos, without the other parties' consent they are a major problem."

"True, and they would demand my daughter's death if this came to be public knowledge. While I do wish to nullify the treaty, I will not do it because of one stupid girl!" As she said the words "stupid girl," she reached behind her with her tail for a wooden crate, which she threw into the shadows. Andrew heard it smash on something like he did before.

"Which is why in the time-honoured tradition of my people, I kidnapped you. Now I am *encouraging* you to marry her, since our people have a saying. What happens within the family, stays within it."

"Which means that her breaking the law would be deemed acceptable, since she would be part of my clan?"

"Precisely. You catch on quickly despite you being human and male."

Clearly Queen Nataganzar didn't have a high opinion of Andrew due to reasons outside his control. Shrugging, he asked, "Why should I? How does this benefit me, or my clan?"

Smiling as best as her face permitted her, it was clear to Andrew that her opinion of him had gone up a small amount. Queen Nataganazar replied, "True. Excuse me while I fetch the bride-to-be, even if she is to be a second wife. We will speak more of this when I return."

As Queen Nataganazar stomped into the shadows, it left Andrew alone for a brief moment, so he used it to look around. He initial assessment of his situation was confirmed when he looked down at his bare legs—he wasn't secured to the chair. What surprised him was that one nearby wall had various weapons, ranging from what appeared to be ancient swords and daggers to the most modern of firearms, even several experimental models he had read about online. *What in the name of God's green earth does a dragon need weapons for?* Andrew thought.

Hearing the scratching of claws on cement, Andrew turned his attention back to the depths of the warehouse he couldn't see, where he now saw Queen Nataganazar dragging what appeared to be a dragon made of living water. Where the queen's scales were clear and well defined, like dark red armor, the other one's colours kept shifting from dark to light blue in waves, and her scales were too small to really see. The other dragon was doing everything possible to cover her face with her wings, and all he really saw was a flash of a brown eye that spoke volumes to him. Like the face of the being who owned it, any sense of self confidence had been beaten out of it centuries ago. Snarling at the younger dragon, Queen Nataganazar commanded her, "Scan his mind, and transform now!"

"No," the young woman said defiantly.

"Do it, or you die!"

"Umm, hate to break up your conversation, but the price of me marrying her?" Andrew interjected.

Waving one clawed paw dismissively, Queen Nataganazar replied, "Oh, isn't that obvious? You will be awarded the rank of Noble within my realm, and that will be all." Slamming the other dragon's head to the ground with enough force Andrew felt it several feet away, she roared, "Scan his mind now, become his ideal mate physically, and transform this instant, young lady!"

"Sorry, your offer isn't enough," Andrew replied.

Turning to face him, the queen said, "Best offer you'll get, given your current position."

Just a touch of a smile was on his face. Andrew didn't say one word as he did what he always did when facing a situation he didn't like. He changed the rules.

Leaning back on the chair, he used the small shard of metal to cut into his plastic bindings, pulling at the same time with all his might to break them. Hearing them snap as the chair hit the floor, he was on his feet in an instant. He grabbed the chair by its legs, and threw it straight at Queen Nataganazar's face. Not waiting to see how it went, he took off like a fat man after an all-you-can-eat food truck towards the wall filled with weapons. He heard the queen roar, "You dare, mortal!?" followed by a blast of flame that flew right by him. He could smell his arm hair being burned off, given how close he was to the burst of flame.

After barely running seventy-five feet, he was already panting; he would have to do more running if he made it out of this mess alive, he thought. Hearing the scratching of claws behind him, he redoubled his efforts, reaching the wall and grabbing the first things he could: a shortsword and pistol. Turning around to face what he assumed would be an enraged charging dragon, he was surprised when he saw she hadn't moved one inch. There appeared to be almost admiration in her eyes when she looked at him. *Had everything been an act he thought, was this all a set up?*

He noted offhand how the blue one's body was smaller, having gone from the size of Queen Nataganazar to the size of a horse, but was still using her wings to block his view of her.

Behind those jagged teeth that looked large enough to rip a jet into scrap iron, the queen said, "It seems your bargaining position has changed, little mortal. State your terms."

Hefting the sword into a better position, Andrew replied, "No marriage today. Instead, she'll live with Erica, myself, and whoever else joins our clan for six months. This will give everyone a better chance to know her. You will pay for the addition to our home to accommodate her, as well as her upkeep during this time."

Nodding her agreement to his terms, Andrew continued, "If her and I should have...carnal relations, we will be considered married. At which point I will become a high-ranking Noble within your empire. Given her transformation, is it safe to assume your people have the ability to prolong mortal life spans via a drug of some sort?"

Despite the distance between them, he heard her reply clearly, "It is."

"I would want that for my clan mates and I, as well as you considering releasing a weakened version to the general public."

"For you and your clan, done. For the public, isn't there enough of your mortals already? There are what, seven billion of you?"

"True, but with declining birth rates in the first world, extended life spans with the extended fertile cycle that would come with it would help them recover."

Nodding, she said, "I'll consider it, but not for the third world. They haven't learned to live in harmony with the planet, or the first world yet. Do you know how many scam calls I get from there?"

Andrew nodded in turn. "Done. This concludes my end. Do you have anything you want from me?" he asked, lifting the gun up.

Shaking her head, Andrew walked towards her now. "If I may ask, what is your daughter's name? I just can't call her 'stupid girl' or something to that effect, can I?"

The queen turned her eyes to glare at the blue dragon who looked less like one every moment. Speaking up though her wings, she said meekly, "My mother named me Victoria, after one of Earth's monarchs she admired when I was but a hatchling."

Close enough to look at each of them directly, he chose to address them both. "Start or end of her reign?"

Queen Nataganazar replied, "Start, naturally. After her husband died, she became a joke of a ruler. Mourning a man for so long. After all, in a true society, women rule, as I have for close to three hundred years."

Andrew added as a mental note that if he was going to represent these people, he needed to learn about them beyond the facts he read online. However, a key word was *if* he took the job. Given his personality, he didn't think he fit the bill. He didn't have a high tolerance for village idiots, and this flaw had gotten him banned from several online games over the years. Maybe he thought with Erica and Bloom's help, he could develop a break on his temper so he could act as a bridge between these two peoples. Hard to believe he would've considered this all mythical two days ago, but it was hard to deny reality when you had no alternative but to live within it.

Taking a more gracious approach, Andrew dropped to one knee in front of Queen Nataganazar. "Your Majesty, I would have your thoughts on the treaty, and I being appointed your people's ambassador to the human would, please."

By now, Victoria had shrunk down to a little over five-foot-eight, but her wings still hid her. Queen Nataganazar replied, "My thoughts are that the treaty should be abolished. Humanity has grown up, and our kind should no longer have to hide from yours. If it means a clashing of species, so be it. It would be a good way to test all of those who live on this world."

Turning, she snarled at Victoria, "No more stalling, girl, retract your wings and reveal yourself to him now!"

Shaking like a leaf, Victoria slowly pulled her wings over her body that now was close to human norm in size, forming an almost skin-tight cover. In an instant, her clothing took form— small black shoes, white ankle shocks, a dark blue pleaded skirt that started right above the knees, a blue sweater that, like her scales, kept shifting from dark to light blue. There were hints of a white golf shirt around the collar of her sweater. Looking to be in her early twenties, she had a small nose and the same brown eyes she'd had as a dragon. Her hair was a few shades lighter blue than her skirt.

"No imagination?" the queen quipped.

"Maybe I thought she'd look good in it?"

Raising as much of an eyebrow as a dragon could, Queen Nataganazar turned to leave. Addressing Andrew one last time, she asked, "Before I leave, I am wondering. What is it with males of your species and their attraction to women with large mammary glands like the ones you had my daughter grow to be your ideal sexual partner?"

"Instinct?"

"As good an answer as I've ever heard," said Queen Nataganazar, almost sounding ready to laugh at Andrew's response. "I will make the arrangements to have your home modified." Bowing her head, Queen Nataganazar said, "And please keep the sword and the gun as a reminder of our meeting."

Walking off into another part of the warehouse, she turned around one last time, "Victoria, please show him and yourself out." With that, the queen vanished from their sight. *Must be night vision that permits her to navigate this place,* thought Andrew. A squeak of a door was heard in the distance, and a vague door-like outline was seen. Taking Andrew by the hand, Victoria guided him towards it, and whispered, "Thank you."

"For what?"

"When I read your mind, you had two ideas. One of your ideal sexual partner, and one that would let me be happy. I hope you don't mind me taking a bit from one to work with the other. It's been over a century since I had a choice like that."

Despite himself, he smirked at that comment. "Hard being the heir apparent?"

"Far from it," she said, looking down at her feet, "Mother would never consider me a worthy heir to the throne. The second I hatched, I was considered a failure."

"Why?"

"Since I am a blue dragon like my great-great-grandfather."

Before Andrew could ask why blues were considered failures, they exited the building and he realized he wasn't in Canada anymore. Instead of maples, oaks, and evergreens, all the trees and plants reflected that of a more tropical climate. Finding his bike and backpack next to the door, he opened up the latter to pick up his cell phone, which is when his jaw dropped. "Erica is going to kill me!"

"How come?"

He held up his cell phone to her. "Look at the time and date!"

Clearly confused, Victoria said, "I don't see the problem, its clearly synchronizing with the cell tower."

"But according to this, I've been gone at least a day!"

Smiling, she replied, "Oh, that. Mother had you flown at Mach Five to a remote island on the other side of the International Date Line." The way she said it made it sound like it was an everyday event.

Andrew had a sudden urge to rub his temples at that rather offhanded remark. "She had me kidnapped, and flown at Mach Five to the middle of nowhere?"

"Yup, this island isn't even on any of your maps," Victoria assured him.

"Great, just great, and how are we supposed to get back home? Not like we can board a flight with a local carrier, and cross international boarders without passports!"

"Oh, that isn't a problem. You could order me to transform, and I could take us underwater to British Columbia. From there, we could arrange transport back home."

Raising an eyebrow, Andrew said, "Order you to transform? Why would I have to do that?"

Holding up one of her hands, Victoria showed Andrew a gold bracelet with a large, blue gem in the middle of it. "Something of a safe guard for when we become involved with mortals. It forces me to keep this form," she said, indicating her body, "until ordered to transform by either you, or someone you authorize to tell me to transform."

Pausing to think, Andrew finally said, "All right, I am going to call Erica, explain things. We'll work from there, cool?"

"Whatever you say, master. Should I step back so I am not in the holo-phone call?"

"Holo-phone call?" *And what's with her calling me 'master'?* he thought.

Reaching for the phone he had in his hand, she explained, "Someone upgraded your phone, so it will deploy both holodrones and cameras. That way it can record and display everything within range on both ends."

After he unlocked his phone, Victoria told him he might want to put it on the ground when he called Erica. Doing as instructed, he was pleasantly surprised when both Erica and Bloom appeared before him. Rushing towards him, Erica went right through him and gave an embarrassed smile. "Sorry, honey."

"Don't worry about it, Erica. Trust me, if you were here with me, I'd want to hug you also. Some things have happened recently, which I need to tell you about."

Something in her eyes told him she wanted to hug him even more as he explained his kidnapping and where he was. Both Bloom and Erica asked at the same time, "Are you all right?!"

"I am," he confirmed. "I was just surprised I was wet when I woke up here."

Stepping into camera range, Victoria introduced herself to Bloom and Erica before explaining things. "When you were first kidnapped, you fell into the pond you were looking at and nearly drowned. When you were brought here, you were barely alive, and Mother had me use my...gifts to heal you. Thing is, I require water to do so, which explains why you were soaking wet when you woke up."

"What's the plan for getting you two home?" asked Erica.

Victoria stepped forward. "If Andrew orders me to, I can transform into my natural form. Once we're in the ocean, I can get us to British Columbia. I assume once we are on land, we can arrange transport to Yanapeachu City."

Bloom asked, "Wait, if you are a dragon, can't you fly?"

Looking a bit embarrassed, Victoria responded, "On my own, yes. With Andrew and cargo, no. It's too heavy for me. Underwater, though, I can carry everything and be in British Columbia in a few hours."

Andrew held a hand up. "Hate to ask this, but you do realize I can't breathe underwater, right? I mean, it is one of my requirements to have air to breathe, otherwise I die, which is a bad thing. And that much sea water would rust my bike out easily, and destroy my cell phone."

Looking a bit ashamed for missing such obvious facts, Victoria merely said, "Oh."

Erica asked, "Don't dragons accommodate other species on their backs all the time in the air? It can't be that hard underwater, can it?"

"It is actually. I could do it if I had the training"—she paused, trying to hold back tears given what she knew about her people—"and I don't, since I am the only Aquos dragon I know of on Earth. I haven't been taught how to do those things." Giving a smile to both Erica and Bloom, she continued, "Unless you two think I should try to learn this with Andrew?"

They shook their heads vigorously, screaming, "No, that is a bad idea!"

"All right, I won't," Victoria said teasingly and laughed.

Erica suggested, "Is there any kind of village nearby to get some supplies? Or maybe you could ferry him on your back?"

"Both those ideas have merit, Erica," Andrew said, looking his wife in the eyes. "Look, I mainly called so you'd know

I am okay and to expect some renovation teams in the morning."

Walking forward towards him, Erica pulled down her blouse so he could see her breasts. "Thank you. Just remember as you travel with her who has your heart," she said as she leaned in for a kiss. Kissing light felt odd to both of them, and looked odd to their companions, who tried to look away. "I mean it, Andrew. Now I can go to bed, and I will see Bloom off."

Getting down on one knee, Andrew asked Bloom to approach him. Resting a hand on one of her shoulders, he said, "Bloom, I want to apologize for not being there today. I understand how important it was for you."

Phasing right through his hand, she wrapped her arms around his neck. "I understand. Besides, it gave me a chance to know Erica better, and I need both of your approval to join the clan," she reminded him.

Smiling, he replied, "I guess you pick up some wisdom when you age slower than the rest of us."

"You certainly do," she said, smiling back at him.

Stepping away, Andrew looked at both women. "Stay safe, both of you, I mean it. I couldn't lose either one of you. I will call you once we reach the west coast."

"We will," they said together as the connection broke off. Turning around, he saw Victoria sniffling, which broke into full-blown crying. "What's wrong?" he asked.

"You meant it? You love them both?"

"I care for them more than I have anyone else in a long time."

"How can you? You only met them a few days ago."

Sighing in contentment, he picked up his smart phone, which he placed in his battered old backpack, and started to walk towards his bike. He explained to her, "You have to understand, Victoria, in both of them I see what I consider the best parts of me present." Motioning for her to follow him down a trail, he continued, "In Erica, I see the fire to push yourself each day, and she's someone I can share my nerd and geekdom stuff with. With Bloom, I see my love of the natural world, despite my job being very technical."

"Okay, so you sleeping with one of them, with the possibility of sleeping with the other is...?"

"It's part physical, and part mental. I am not like most men. For me to sleep with someone, it has to be something deeper for it to happen."

"So, it won't happen with us on this tropical island?"

"Not even if your mother had a million dollars," and for some reason a very old song Andrew knew started to play in his head as they headed towards the sea.

Doing her best to keep it in, Victoria knew her mother had over a quadrillion dollars, which she could only assume was over a million. She honestly didn't know if it was.

****

Once Andrew hung up, Erica got down and hugged Bloom; they had both been worried about Andrew being out of touch. "He's all right!" they said in unison, and couldn't help but smile. Getting down on Bloom's level, Erica reached for her purse on a nearby table. "Bloom, I am not returning your gift to us, but I do want to give you something before you go, all right?"

"Okay."

Pulling out several bills, she handed them to the gnome. "This isn't any indication that you are too poor to join this clan, or you have nothing to offer us. This is a gift so when you join us, you can make yourself look like the princess you were, and will be again if I have anything to say about it."

Looking at the money in her hand, Bloom replied, "You mean that, don't you?"

"I do."

Hugging Erica, Bloom said, "It's a long drive back to Gnome Express."

Watching the gnome walk herself out the door, Erica had several thoughts. The road to redemption was not easy with either gnomes or dwarves, or to reclaim her birthright.

However, with a strong family, all things were possible. As Erica closed the door and prepared for bed, she couldn't help but also reflect on how happy the gnome appeared to be.

****

If Erica thought Bloom was happy, she was severely underestimating the gnome's state of mind. Bloom knew it was a long drive home, and was ecstatic. This was the first time that a First Wife had approved of her, and she was extremely attracted to both her possible mates. This was more than she could ever have imagined or hoped for. Maybe after all her setbacks, she was moving forward in life.

Pulling up to Gnome Express, her mood started to plunge. Unlike Erica's home, which had so much life around it, Gnome Express was in the middle of an industrial park. Parking her car, Jerry was outside waiting for her with a snarl on his face. "Well, if it isn't the finest biological teleporter in Gnome Express. Have fun?"

Looking at the clock, a dejected Bloom pointed out, "Jerry, it's late, I just want to go to bed."

Commanding her to empty her purse before him, she did. Picking up the money, he began to stuff it into his pockets. "Think you could hide this money from me, did you?"

"No, Jerry," she said, looking down.

"You know the company regs—even if you find a cent outside the office, it belongs to Gnome Express."

"To enhance and build up our fine and outstanding company, all money must go to the head of the company," she said, finishing his statement. She also knew it was a crock. No matter how hard, how dangerous, or how well paying the job was, the shares she and her sisters received were so slim as to be drastically below the poverty level.

Technically, the car she drove was company property. She didn't even own a basic cell phone. It was all she could afford on her "generous" compensation package from him—

some plants for the room she shared with Hotwire, along with her clothing and toiletries.

"Put out your arms, now!" he commanded her.

"Okay." At this time of night, and given how sleepy she was, he could command her to frog march to Mars and she'd have done it. In a flash, a knife was in his hand, and he slashed through her blouse, leaving matching cuts on both arms. Following up, he kicked her to the ground. "That's for leaving me to handle the Werewolf kids during the move while you were out having fun all day!"

Not bothering to say another word to her, he walked away, filled with rage, while all Bloom could do was hold back tears as she shoved the contents of her purse back within it and off the cold, damp cement floor. She knew if he heard her crying, he'd just beat her for fun until she stopped.

Making her way back to the small room she shared with Hotwire, the other gnome stopped what she was doing on her work bench to greet, "How did your—" but the question never even finished leaving her mouth as she ran to get the first aid kit. Looking over her shoulder, Hotwire realized how deep the cuts were, so she changed plans and grabbed an epidermal regenerator she'd made from spare parts that she used for emergencies like this. Applying it to one arm and then the next, she comforted Bloom as they sat on one of the two beds in the room. "There, there, sis, we'll patch you up."

"Thanks, Hotwire."

"We've got to get out from Jerry—the sooner, the better!"

"I know. A few days ago, he threatened to remove my..." Bloom was so traumatized by his threat that she couldn't finish saying it. "We can't get away from him." She was on the verge of tears. "When we were exiled, he became head of the family until we marry out."

"It doesn't mean what he does is right. If we were humans, we wouldn't have to put up with his abuse towards any of us."

Hugging her sister tight, Hotwire asked Bloom how her date went.

"Great, only Andrew wasn't there. But the great news is Erica approves of me!"

Confused, Hotwire asked, "Erica is who?"

"The First Wife."

"So, if she approves, you're as good as in!" Punching her sister as gently as she could in the shoulder, Hotwire said, "Nice going, sis!" Walking over to their computer, she began to type something in. "No pressure, sis, but I think I know a way you can get us away from Jerry."

Walking up and joining Hotwire, she asked, "How?"

Pulling up a Wiki article, she explained, "It's an ancient gnome tradition, where if one family member marries into a family, she or he can ask for blood siblings to be accepted into the new family."

Both of them had a certain amount of trust in Wiki, given how many times information was crossed referenced on the site. "But Hotwire, this tradition is fifteen hundred years old! Who knows the last time it was used."

"It's still a tradition, Bloom. It's still on the books, and we are part-gnome."

"But it pre-dates the accords that bind all non-humans by five hundred years!"

Smiling, Hotwire pointed out, "Loophole in the accords—even if a tradition hasn't been used in centuries, it can be used at the discretion of the clan and the people involved. Question is, do you think they'd go for it?"

For a moment, Bloom thought of what she knew of both Erica and Andrew. Andrew, who stopped along the way back home to help her bury roadkill. Erica, who showed her a bit of her business today. Andrew, who had no problem sharing the driving back home, and Erica, who, besides performing great cunnilingus on her, accepted her own inexperience when she tried to return the favor on the centaur. Without hesitation, she said yes to Hotwire's question.

"Then, when marriage comes up, you know what to do."

"I do," Bloom said firmly. Giving her sister a hug from behind, she continued, "Thank you, and good night, Hotwire."

"Good night."

Changing for bed, Bloom went to sleep with something she hadn't had in ages: genuine hope that tomorrow, the future would be better—not just for her, but for her sisters as well. Despite what Jerry thought of her and other people.

Chapter 5

Bloom and Hotwire were both woken by Jerry shouting, "Wake up, ladies, we got work, up, up, up!" He hammered on the doors with who knew what. It was enough to wake the dead, and given how Sherry preferred to sleep in a coffin, it wasn't overstating the fact. Looking at the clock, Bloom saw it had barely been three hours since she had fallen asleep. Looking across from her, she saw Hotwire was in the same level of disarray she was—wild bedhead and all—but, unlike Bloom, who preferred a bed, Hotwire preferred a hammock. Getting out of bed, the two gnomes started to walk down the hall in their nightgowns. Hotwire's was an old jumpsuit she'd modified years ago, while Bloom's was something she'd bought years ago.

Entering the meeting room, they saw Sherry sitting down at the table already. Her black hair covering her eyes, she looked like the epitome of the living dead. Sitting down to join her, both Hotwire and Bloom tried to cover their eyes. The light seemed to burn into all their eyes, except Jerry, who seemed awake and chipper. Mind you, that that didn't explain his sense of fashion. Today, he had decided to go with an orange full-length shirt, and what humans had called "parachute pants" in mauve of all things. Despite all his sisters barely being awake, he hadn't bothered to make coffee.

Smiling, he said, "Good morning, ladies!" His smile seemed so wide it was like his face was ready to break in two.

Hotwire would've thrown something at him, but the table was bare except for a few sheets of paper. "Jerry, have you been doing cocaine again?"

"No, I have not been doing cocaine again!" he said in a rapid-fire fashion.

Looking at the clock that hung above his head, she pointed out, "It's three a.m., we should all be asleep!"

Raising a finger as he began to walk around the table, Jerry replied, "Ah, but not every non-human sleeps at three a.m., and I just finished working out a moving deal for a nice clan with a few Slimes in it."

All three of them said in unison, "Slimes. Eww, gross."

Rubbing her eyes, still trying to wake up, Bloom asked, "Fom where to where, Jerry? Since we all know Slimes aren't usually up at three in the morning." Shouting, she added, "And some of us need our beauty sleep!"

Stopping so he was right across from Bloom, both of Jerry's hands slammed on the table as he shouted back, "Watch your tone with me, missy! I run this company from top to bottom!"

"Yes, Jerry," she replied, shrinking back a bit.

"The move is from Kingston, Ontario to Tampico, Mexico, so bring your swimsuits, ladies. Once we're done, you can enjoy some R and R."

Sounding like a zombie, Sherry inquired, "How long?"

"Maybe an hour, two. Depends how long it takes to get there." Turning to face Hotwire, he asked, "All right, Hotwire, status on the cloak, expanded fuel tanks, and interphasing matter transducer?"

Doing her best to keep her head up, Hotwire replied, "Shot, nowhere near ready, and the transducer is on its last legs."

"So, we need to drive like normal unless we want to pay the extra fees to use the non-human roads."

Everyone present knew how cheap Jerry was. He would never pay to use those roads, or for the parts Hotwire required to do the work he wanted done. She was always visiting junkyards to scavenge for materials the business required, from the van to even the paper in their printers.

The girls reluctantly got up as one, knowing that was Jerry's way of closing up the meeting.

****

Bloom was still wearing her nightgown as she entered the main bay where a majority of the company's supplies were kept. Goosebumps went up all over her body from the cold; Jerry didn't want to give Hotwire the money she needed to properly repair the environmental controls, so it was usually either super hot or super cold here. For all her technical skills, Hotwire had yet to find the parts or programming she needed on the web to do that kind of work for free.

Wandering into the back, she knew she would need special supplies to help move slimes, from hologenerators, stasis field generators, calibration gear. She was so involved in her work, she didn't hear Jerry until he was practically behind her.

There was a smile on his lips that almost screamed crazy, matching the look in his eyes. Her sword was in his hand, and he dragged it along the cement floor, raising sparks as he slowly walked towards her. "No need to bother yourself, little sister. Big brother is going to move the slimes all by himself." His voice was filled with sarcasm.

Backing away from him, she stammered out, "Jerry— Jerry, what's wrong?"

Raising the sword off the floor, he said calmly, "I know about the research, and how your date went, and I am here to stop it." Raising the sword, he advanced, cackling; it was like when Jerry got them exiled years ago, thought Bloom. He had been meeting an elf princess to secure an alliance, and no one knew what happened. All they knew were the results—that the princess had sexual intercourse and was killed, while Jerry had claimed self-defence. He'd said that the princess had forced herself on him, and that he had beat her off, accidentally killing her in the process.

The only way to keep the peace was to exile Jerry, and his mother and sisters since they had all believed him at the time. Looking into his eyes now, Bloom couldn't believe how wrong they had been. The abuse he had done to all of them over the years had been a precursor to this moment. Even the casual violence earlier this evening should have been a warning.

She kept backing up, her heart beating so fast in fear that she felt it was going to rip out of her chest. For some reason, she thought of Andrew and Erica, and the rest was easy.

Instead of continuing to back up and let him butcher her, she charged at him head on, and sucker-punched him square in the jaw. Sending him flying, an I-beam stopped him, knocking him out cold. Pulling her sword out of his hand with care, she placed it out of reach as she clinically began to beat him. Careful not to administer a killing blow, it was like she was divided into two parts—one that knew how to beat Jerry within an inch of his life, and the part of her that would always see him as family, which meant killing him wasn't possible for her.

She wasn't just administering this beating for revenge after years of abuse, but for her sisters and her future family. Mess with any of them, and be warned, you will face her wrath, she thought.

She would never know how long it took, but by the time she stopped beating him, she was red in the face, panting, sweat running down her face. Her hair was soaked as it hung loosely off of her. She finally stopped as the clinical part that had been handling the beating considered Jerry sufficiently hurt. Looking up, she saw Hotwire and Sherry watching from one of the walkways, both of them still in their nightwear. "Yes?" she asked.

Smiling and giving her a thumbs up, Hotwire said, "Good job! What's next?"

"Why ask me?"

Leaning over the rail, Hotwire replied, "Since, from the looks of things, you broke every bone in Jerry's body twice."

"Your point?" Looking at the damage she had inflicted on her brother, plans began to roll through her mind.

"You rock, so you lead! We'll follow you! Won't we, Sherry?"

"Yeah," Sherry said. She almost sounded awake.

Looking up at them, Bloom ordered, "All right, we have two hours to pack up everything we need. I want a phone for Jerry here!" Kicking him in the ribs, she continued, "To call nine-one-one an hour after that." Clapping her hands together to emphasize her point, saying, "All right, ladies, let's roll!"

With that, the gnome sisters began to scramble. None of them knew if this was the start or the end of things, but what they did know was that things were changing.

****

Despite the island Andrew and Victoria were on being off the map, Queen Nataganazar employed enough people on it to justify a motel six—as in it was a motel with six rooms, none of which had two beds, forcing Andrew and Victoria to share, given how the other rooms were taken. He was grateful for the fact that despite how bare the room was, the staff had been able to dig up an old USB cable to charge his phone as he slept. He half suspected he'd need it more than ever in the future.

Given how he didn't have much in the way of clothes with him, and the hotel lacked normal human sleepwear for sale, he had opted to wear his underwear to sleep in. He recommended Victoria do the same. Then she had insisted on sleeping naked, explaining that even though she looked human, she was still a dragon, and dragons slept naked. As a compromise, he informed her she could sleep naked, but asked that she disrobe under the sheets, which she agreed to.

Until Erica and him had a chance to talk, and get to know Victoria, he didn't want to give her a hint of accepting her as a wife.

Even with their compromise, he still had wet dreams—only natural under the circumstances. The woman in play kept shifting; sometimes it was someone he knew in the distant past, other times fictional characters. Even the positions changed, but every time he'd have his orgasm, it would start all over again, which was weird. It was like he couldn't find any sexual release, and something was stopping him from waking up.

By now, he had lost count of how many times he had cum in his dream, but somehow, he finally did, and it all made sense. Even in his half-dozy sleep state, he recognized a blue head of hair that was firmly between his legs, even if he was lying on his side. "Victoria!" he shouted.

Tilting her head up to face him, she gave a meek wave before pulling back to release his cock from her mouth with a *plop,* saying, "Uh, good morning?"

Slapping his forehead, he asked, "What did you think you were doing?"

"Stopping you from wetting the bed like a child. I mean, I let it go the first time. However, after that, I put my mouth around your penis so you wouldn't wet the bed further." Clearly, she didn't think to wake Andrew up, or to try and somehow get something to soak the mess up. "Which is why I put my mouth around your cock to clean it up before you could wet the bed. Why did you keep doing it, by the way? Don't you have any bladder control?"

"Why didn't you wake me up instead of giving me blow jobs?"

"What's a blow job?" she asked. Smiling, she added, "Besides, sometimes my saliva has a mild sedative in it. It comes in handy when trying to heal someone who is injured."

"But I wasn't hurt." At least this explained why he hadn't woken up.

"If you are wetting the bed at your age, you do have problems," she told him. This was turning out to be one of the stranger conversations Andrew had ever had.

Sighing, he replied, "It's a normal, healthy reaction for a human male in the circumstances we're in." This was not a conversation he wanted to have before having a cup of coffee. "Just in case you are wondering, that wasn't urine—that was semen you were sucking up."

Pushing herself up to join him at the head of the bed, she started to automatically cuddle with him. In some ways, she was like a young animal trying to learn how to do what the older ones did naturally. He didn't realize until now how beautiful she was until she was up here with him, and how quickly his cock became erect. "You are doing it again," she said. "And what circumstances are we in, and what's semen?" Lowering herself a bit, she tried to position her head under his chin, and lay a hand and breast on his chest.

"You really don't know?"

"No," she said, like she had no clue the effect she was having on him. Part of Andrew wanted to push her away, part of him said it was too early to care, and a final part wanted to pin her to the bed and fuck her brains out. Then again, given how she appeared to be an airhead, that wouldn't be right, he thought. Something felt wrong in him for even considering having sex with her at this stage of their relationship. Even if just glancing at her chest got him going.

Sighing, he started, "We are—" before interrupting himself as it clicked that he could see his own cock. "Where is my underwear?"

Pushing her head under his chin, Victoria absentmindedly reached out to stroke his cock. "Human body, dragon strength. I sort of ripped them off of you when I wanted to get to your penis to try and stop you from wetting the bed."

Pushing her hand away from his cock, he replied, "Where was I? Oh, yes, we're both naked in bed and you made yourself to look like my dream woman. It's natural for my penis to become like that. And as for what semen is, it's what males produce that, when combined with eggs inside a woman, creates a child."

Pushing herself up, she looked down at him, shocked. "Are you saying I am going to be a mother? I need to make a roost, like now!" Scrambling out of the bed, Victoria started to run around the room in a mad panic, unable to determine what she wanted to do next.

Getting out of bed himself, Andrew said, "Calm down, Victoria. Swallowing all that semen will not make you pregnant!" *At least, not if you work like all other women,* he thought.

"It won't?" One of her blue eyebrows shot up to illustrate her confusion.

"It won't," he confirmed. "Unless my semen ends up in contact with your eggs, you will not become pregnant."

"Oh, that's a relief." She slowed down a bit from her earlier rushed pace.

Rubbing his forehead, Andrew thought this was not a conversation one expected to have with a 150-odd-year-old dragon first thing in the morning. "Why don't you hit the showers? We'll grab some breakfast and see how we can get off the island without going through immigration back in Canada."

As she walked away, she asked, "I just have one request of you before I shower."

"And that is?"

"Would you mind shaving down some of your body hair a bit, please?"

"I'll consider it."

Somehow in his soul, Andrew knew that this was going to be one of those days where he had wished he had stayed in bed. Correct that, stay with his fellow humans. Maybe this was why the government signed the no-contact treaty—too many days like this. Grabbing his black t-shirt off the floor, he saw his phone flashing with an incoming call. "Holophone on, waist up only," he said as he answered.

Andrew admitted he found it weird to see people as holograms while talking with them, but it was also a good way to cut down on people using their phones while driving. "Good morning, Andrew speaking."

Bloom, Sherry, and Hotwire were on their knees as they took shape, as did Erica, who appeared to be sitting behind her desk at the office.

Bloom was the first one to speak. "Andrew, I apologize for waking you up so early. My sisters and I have an urgent request of Erica and yourself."

"What's the matter, Bloom?" Erica asked.

"I know we haven't known each other that long, and neither of you have spent any real time with my sisters. However, I am asking that you accept me as one of Andrew's wives, and we are invoking the gnomish ritual of Ratatitus." Adding in an urgent tone of voice, she continued, "We need this done today."

While Andrew was lost on the ritual, Erica knew about it since she asked, "Your sisters know what that means, right? And you are not invoking it to avoid a capital crime case, are you?"

"They know and accept it, and we are not trying to avoid the legal death penalty. We're invoking it since we fear for our lives."

"Well, I don't," piped in Andrew. "Someone mind explaining what the ritual of Ratatitus means?"

Getting up, Hotwire walked towards Andrew. "You know how we as a people are very family oriented?"

"Yes?"

The red-headed gnome said, "Ratatitus is a fifteen-hundred-year-old ritual where blood relatives swap family obligations, if one marries into another. It also means"—she started to blush a bit—"that if we wanted children or a sexual encounter, we'd go to you for it. Fathering our children or sharing our bed would be entirely your choice."

It looked like his gut was right about how today would be, thought Andrew. "Wait, wouldn't that mean I'd have my three wives?"

"No," Erica corrected him. "Hotwire and Sherry would be more like harem women, extended members of the family. We would be under an obligation to protect them, and they'd be outside their old family rules." Focusing on Bloom, she said, "The question is why, Bloom. Why seek out our protection and ask to join our family so urgently?"

Bloom, Sherry, and Hotwire started to lay it all out to Erica and Andrew about Jerry. About the mysterious death of the princess, a mother who drank herself to death, about all the abuse he'd laid on them once he became the head of the clan decades ago.

With everything Andrew heard, he became more and more enraged. This news, combined with the unexpected blow jobs, made coffee a secondary thing this morning to wake up. If by the time their tale ended, Bloom hadn't admitted to beating Jerry within a millimetre of his life, Andrew would have done it himself. To think he considered Jerry a possible friend in the non-human world was proof of wrong first impressions. Barely seeing clearly, he asked, "Why not go to the police about this?"

"Our people don't have any laws against domestic abuse, Andrew," Erica replied.

"Oh." He clearly had a lot to learn still about these people. By now, Victoria had returned from her shower and watched the conversation from behind Andrew, out of camera view.

"And when Jerry recovers, if we aren't married out, he'll hunt us down and kill us! Given how we would be still considered part of his family at the time, he'd get away with it."

It was a lot to take in, thought Andrew; he seemed to be thinking that a lot recently. "Bloom, is there a way Erica and I can talk privately for just a few moments?"

"Sure." She stepped back and in the place of herself, Sherry, and Hotwire, the words "standing by" appeared. Victoria took that as a clue to step back into the bathroom to give Andrew and Erica some privacy.

Andrew sat down on the bed and the holograms readjusted themselves so Erica and Andrew were face to face. "Well, good morning, honey," he said meekly.

"I know what you're thinking, Andrew, and it is a lot to take in. The good thing is, if Bloom is telling the truth, it isn't a capital crime. I do believe her."

Sighing, he looked down. "Same here. I was hoping for us to get more in sync before getting into another shotgun wedding." Looking up at her, he said firmly, "Not that I regret marrying you for a second!"

Getting up from behind her desk, Erica put her hands over his. "Andrew, my love, what does your heart tell you?"

"Do it. The warrior part of me cannot let innocents be put in harm's way."

Andrew saw Erica give him a huge smile and try to kiss him before saying, "That is one of the many reasons why I proposed to you. I knew about your warrior nature before we even kissed."

Smiling back at her, he said, "Just remember who beat you. How do we get them off standby?"

"Oh, simple." Addressing the phone, Erica said, "Take other users off standby."

In a flash, Bloom, Sherry, and Hotwire were seen, all of them displaying clearly nervous signs. Bloom rushed towards Erica and Andrew. "And the decision is?"

Clearing his throat, Andrew got up and kneeled before Bloom. "If you are willing to join our Clan, I, Andrew, husband of this clan, propose to you, Bloom." Shifting his eyes towards Erica, he said, "We will honour the ritual of Ratatitus."

Erica now approached Bloom. "As first wife of this clan, I also ask you join this clan, and agree to honour the ritual of Ratatitus."

Even in her holographic form, Andrew saw the tears of joy form in Bloom's eyes. "Thank you, thank you, you have no idea what this means for my sisters and I."

"I take that as a yes?"

"Of course, silly!" Much to his surprise, as Bloom went to hug him, Hotwire tried also. Getting close to his ear, he heard her whisper, "Thank you."

"I'd normally offer you a ring, Bloom, but that's sort of hard via hologram, and do you people do engagement rings?"

"No, we don't, due to the fact we don't have fancy human weddings," replied Erica. "We also have a problem that maybe you can help us out with, please?" All three gnomes replied "sure" at the same time. "Andrew is on an island in the middle of the Pacific, and is still trying to secure passage back to Canada without going through customs."

"I assume getting back the way he came is out of the question?" asked Hotwire.

"Naturally, Hotwire," replied Erica.

"Why not just use his holophone as a homing beacon? We can teleport him back home off of its signal."

"Yeah, but Hotwire..." Andrew began, at which point, depending on your understanding of physics and computers, the conversation broke down to bytes, wave signals, and, at one point, Bloom mentioned something about neuro-transmitters on a sigma scale. Everyone not involved with the conversation stood back as the three techies talked it out and it degenerated into language the others didn't understand. It was like they were talking some separate language instead of English. It wasn't until they heard Bloom say, "All right, that works, Andrew. Hotwire, how soon until the app is ready?"

"Five to ten minutes, going to need to modify the code and upload it to Andrew's phone."

Turning to Victoria, Andrew said, "Victoria, could you go the front desk and buy, say, twenty D batteries?"

While working on a tablet she had dug up, Hotwire said, "Better make it twenty-five, maybe thirty."

Looking confused, Victoria asked, "What's a battery, and what's a D-sized kind?"

"It's a type of energy cell. They'll know what I am talking about. Given your relationship to the Queen, hopefully they'll just charge it to the room."

"Okay," said the dragon princess as she left the room, still naked. Stepping back for a moment, Andrew used that time to put on his shorts, shoes, and socks.

Erica walked over to him. "What is going on precisely, Andrew?"

Getting up, he walked over to the phone to enable full view. "What's going on, Erica, is that Hotwire is modifying an app. It'll use my phone to get basic information to the central transporter. As it teleports Victoria, it'll drain the batteries she's carrying, providing the incoming power it requires to move her."

"What about you, and your supplies?"

"Once we confirm Victoria is done, we scan my stuff and I use the hotel's power to get the lock, and repeat." Snapping his fingers as an idea came to him, he turned to the gnome sisters. "Actually, Sherry, Bloom, Hotwire, I have a favour to ask."

"Yes?" they all said in sync. It was funny to both Erica and Andrew how much had happened in this brief conversation.

"Any chance you could dragon-sit? Victoria is nice, but a little bit of an airhead. I'd like to spend some time with Erica before the wedding. Speaking of which, where are we holding it?"

Erica replied, "Actually, the ritual of Ratatitus requires it be at our home. I say the living room."

Everyone nodded their consent, and Sherry actually spoke. "And I see no problem with us dragon-sitting as we prepare for the wedding."

"Thank you, Sherry, it means a lot to us. You three do realize that as members of this family you will have to pull your own weight."

Eyes focused on the tablet, Hotwire said, "Of course. Besides, part of the ritual means we collectively get three quarters of Gnome Express. We might not be ultra rich, but enough to get something started."

Andrew had been busy making sure everything he and Victoria had brought was laid out; unlike a typical transport, if it couldn't be seen, it couldn't be teleported. Looking to Hotwire, he asked, "Status?"

"We're good, transmitting the app now to your phone."

Which is precisely when Victoria re-entered the motel room carrying the batteries. Looking to everyone, she asked, "What do I do with them?"

"Hang onto them and stand still. Same with you, Andrew," instructed Hotwire. "All right, here goes nothing," she said as she pressed the button on her phone. In an instant, all the drones he could see focused on he and Victoria as they were teleported away.

****

The wood panelling of Erica's office replaced the bland walls of the motel Andrew had been staying in. Just as he formed, he was forced to bend over, vomiting all over the floor. At the same time, he felt his shorts fall down around his ankles, like he had suddenly lost a lot of weight. He could hear Erica rushing behind him to help him up. "Are you okay, Andrew?"

Forcing himself up, he felt dizzy. "Just not what I expected."

"Well, you are the first human to be teleported."

"True." Looking around the office, he saw all his stuff had arrived intact, including his mountain bike. Stepping out of his shorts, he walked over to the bike and gave it an affectionate pat. "You know, I think I could take this thing through the gates of hell and back, and she'd still be in one piece."

He heard Erica chuckle behind him. "So what happened to cause your shorts to fall down like that?"

Turning around, he walked back to her. "Remember how we spoke about the teleporter needing extra energy?"

"Yes."

"Fat is energy. Bloom, Hotwire, and I accounted for that when we did the calculations." Giving his now-taut belly a pat, he said, "Beats liposuction on getting weight off." Erica could feel Andrew mentally shift gears. "Are we doing the right thing? And how do you know about this ritual of Ratatitus?"

Picking up one of his hands, the Centaur reassured him. "Yes, my love, we are doing the right thing. As for how I know of the ritual, it's because in order to earn the right to be First Wife, I needed to know all the rituals of all the different species. It's part of my job as First Wife in our clan to lead them."

Smirking, he said, "Even the human ones?"

"I'll leave that to you," she replied affectionately.

She gave him a tender kiss on the cheek before the door to her office opened up and Sabrina slid in. "Erica, store number eight is on the line and do you—" She stopped dead where she stood as she took it all in. Thankfully, Erica's desk blocked Andrew from the waist down. "Oh," she said.

Andrew held up a hand. "Could you give me a moment, please?"

Sabrina turned around while Andrew got his shorts back on—maybe someone could loan him a belt, he thought. Since Sabrina couldn't see him, he said, "It's safe now."

Turning back around and sliding forward, Sabrina extended her hand towards him. "Hello, you must be Andrew. I am Sabrina, daughter of clan Zyyumizika. Currently unattached, and seeking a new clan." The second she said the last part, she regretted it, given the look she received from Erica.

Shaking her hand firmly, he replied, "A pleasure, Sabrina."

Turning to Erica, Sabrina said, "Erica, store number eight's manager just walked out in a snit, and the latest flour shipment hasn't arrived at central distribution yet. I'd follow up on it with Lissazuk, but she's out sick. And we need that flour to make fresh goods at several locations for tomorrow morning."

Rubbing her temples, Erica sighed, and Andrew knew precisely how she felt. "All right, Sabrina, I'll get right on it. How about you show Andrew around the office, and introduce him to the staff?"

Giving them a large smile, the Lamian took Andrew's hand. "With pleasure, Erica."

Sabrina tried to pull Andrew close to her as she led him out of Erica's office, saying to him, "Even after seeing Erica's ring and the footage, I thought it was a rumour that Erica had married a human, but here you are."

"Here I am," he said.

Despite preferring to work remotely, Andrew had been in enough offices over the years to get a sense of things. To his surprise, it looked normal. Swap different skin colors for races, adjust the female to male ratio, and it looked like any other office.

The only time things got weird for him was when some of the women introduced themselves as unattached and seeking a new clan. He made a mental note to follow up with Erica what it meant when women told him they were unattached and seeking a new clan. Did that mean they were single and hitting on him? Announcing their social status as normal? So much to learn, like being thrown into the deep end of the pool and told to swim.

Walking up to an open air duct, Sabrina shouted up into it, "Archie, I have someone down here for you to meet."

From the air duct, Andrew heard, "No time, Sabi, major techno mojo problem here. Need to work on it before the boss lady asks me for an update."

Looking up, Andrew offered, "Maybe I could help?"

Some muttering could be heard—including the words "newb" and "greenhorn"—as Archie descended down into the office on a silk string from his spider end. Despite his rather negative mood, it turned around the second Archie saw Andrew. "All right, I was wrong, bro. Maybe you can help. Let me check your background." Passing a tablet from one of his rear legs to his front human arms, he took a photo of Andrew, and watched the screen intently. "Hmm, not much of a code monkey guy, but you are a solid hardware guy."

Turning to Sabrina, he continued, "Get Andrew a tablet. I'll get him prepped. Unless you think Erica will have a problem with me hijacking him for some work?"

Sliding away, Sabrina said, "Sure, she might find it a bit fun to know he's working for us." Making sure Andrew could hear her, she added, "And I'll go get your bike."

Archie and Andrew went over what work was required where, so Archie could focus on problems at head office. Archie even showed Andrew how to use the tablet to interface with their systems. Once Andrew was prepared, he took off to help out with some of the problems in the field.

****

It wasn't until the work day was done that Erica came out of her office, seeing only a handful of people left working. Several times she had asked Sabrina or other people who came to her what Andrew had been doing, or where he was. They had all been rather ambiguous about it. Now that she was preparing to head home for the day, she wanted to know where her husband was. She would've called him directly, but a side effect of the hacked-together teleporter booster was that it had fried Andrew's phone.

Walking up to Sabrina's desk, she made sure she could be heard before saying, "Sabrina, you know I am your boss, right?"

"Yes."

"So answer me this rather direct question." Sounding as sweet as possible, she asked, "Where is my husband?"

Looking up from her computer, the Lamian responded in a rather offhanded manner, "Oh, he's in the showers. He's been helping Archie out all day. He was cycling between sites doing the hardware work, so Archie could work the code end stuff from here."

"Wait, he went to the showers? The office communal showers?" Several people who worked at Centaur Café preferred to get to the office by means other than public or private transport, so they used the showers before work to look presentable.

Images of her single female staff members ambushing Andrew in the showers on the chance of having an encounter with him filled Erica's head, until she heard Sabrina burst out laughing. "Don't worry, Erica. Andrew took the back way in; no one knows he's in there except Archie and I."

"How did you know what I was thinking?"

"Part of the job of being your assistant—know what the boss is thinking before she does, so you can get ahead of her."

"True. So how did he do?"

"Archie is as happy as a spider that landed several fat flies at the same time."

"That's good to hear. Do you think it's wise he's still doing this kind of work? Since the High Council wants him to be our Ambassador to the human world to work out a new treaty, among other duties."

The Lamian pushed herself up from sitting position to standing so she was eye to eye with her Centaurian boss. She took a moment to adjust her glasses before saying, "I think if he's going to be our ambassador to the human world, he needs more than a diverse clan. He needs to work, play, he needs to really be one of us."

"True. How did people in public react?"

If anyone had the pulse of Centaur Café, it was Sabrina. "Oh, some women tried to woo him, cops ignored him since they scanned his wedding ring, several people stared at him. He took it all in stride like he's used to being this mysterious lord."

Nodding with approval, Erica replied, "Good to hear," giving her assistant a light pat on the shoulder. "Thanks for the information. I'll go collect him and head home for the night."

Giving her boss a smile, Sabrina replied, "Don't go too wild tonight, he's had a big day."

Smirking, Erica said, "No promises. Night," holding up one of her hands with her fingers crossed. Sure enough, she heard the company shower going, and Andrew was in there. He was so lost in thought that he didn't hear her approach him. She could look at those legs all day and it still wouldn't be enough. Slowing her advance, she put her hands over his eyes, gently licking his ear before saying, "Guess who?"

"Erica," he said as he turned around to face her, kissing her on impulse and wrapping his arms around her.

Kissing him back, she then backed up a bit and replied, "Smart man. You almost done?"

"Yeah, just need to dry off." Stepping out of the shower, he grabbed a towel hanging on the wall and wrapped it around his waist, commenting, "Been a while since I could do this." Grabbing another towel, he started to use it to dry off. Once done, he stepped into one of the changing rooms which felt very large to him. Must be for beings with more than two legs, he thought as he started to get dressed.

He heard Erica say to him, "You know we are married? There is no need to change in private."

"I know, but I'm still a bit sensitive about full nudity in front of anyone."

Smiling, she said back, "I'll break you of that habit yet."

Stepping out of the changing room, Erica heard that clicking noise she'd heard before coming from his shoes. "If you don't mind me asking, what's causing that clicking noise?"

Pausing for a moment, he raised a leg, pointing to a tab of metal sticking out from under his shoes. "They allow me to use more of my leg muscles when cycling so I achieve higher speeds."

"Ah, good to know."

Stepping outside the office with Erica close behind, Andrew threw his backpack on as he got on his bike. Erica asked, "Is it normal for humans to have so many pairs of shoes?"

They started on their way home. Sounding surprised, he asked, "You went through my stuff, and you are asking about my shoes?"

"I did no—"

Interrupting her, he said after a brief laugh, "Erica, I am not mad. We're married, I expect you to go through my stuff. Just don't get judgmental about the more...adult parts of my collection."

"Yes, I did check out some of your things, and you'll turn a blind eye to mine? At least until we have a chance to clean house?"

"Consider it done. For the record, my shoe collection is rather modest."

"Good to know. First time I've lived with a humanoid. Centaurs don't really use shoes."

As the conversation shifted, Andrew's mind semi-automated what he was saying, something an ex of his had said she hated about him. She had called it his "chess master," like she never had his full undivided attention.

Just thinking about things, he realized he had always felt out of touch with the human world when he was growing up. As his peers became obsessed with the latest fashion craze, he was more focused on the latest novel. As they had swooned over the latest Hollywood mega star, he was gaga for tech. In essence, he had never been normal; he barely batted an eye as he saw a dragonewt apparently talking up some fat woman who was also part lizard.

Maybe this is why I belong here, he thought. He and Erica kept talking as they headed home until she said something he missed. "Are you going to accept the job of Ambassador from the High Council?" she repeated.

"Sorry, lost in thought. Erica, you do realize I resigned from a job due to 'personal problems' a few years ago, right? At least, that is what Human Resources called it." His voice filled with sarcasm when he mentioned Human Resources. "I call it backing the wrong horse. My manager was an ass." Realizing what he'd said, he promptly apologized.

"No need, Andrew. I might be part horse," she said, affectionately patting her other end, "but I don't take offence at you using that slang. To that point, I did not know you had other jobs."

"Part of the joy of being a human millennial—always working multiple jobs trying to get ahead." Focusing on the road in front of them, they made a turn onto what appeared to be a dirt trail that he knew led to Erica's home. "Thing is, when I resigned, I called my boss every name in the book. I didn't just burn my bridges with the company, I nuked them and salted the soil."

"Your point?"

"Ambassadors are supposed to be nice, level-headed people! I am the kind of person who, when he fights, doesn't aim to hurt his foes, he tries to kill them. Metaphorically speaking."

Then, much to his surprise, Erica started to laugh. "Did I say something funny?" he asked.

"No, just thinking that maybe it's because of how you resigned that the High Council wants you for the job."

Despite being new to these woods, Andrew felt a familiarity knowing he was coming home, and extended a hand to Erica. "And how would the High Council know how I resigned?"

Gripping his hand, she replied, "Do you think human governments are the only one watching everyone?"

"True, but I am such small potatoes."

"Once you and I became married, it was easy enough information to dig up." Both of them laughed at her bad joke. "Which explains why they were able to authorize the addition to our home so quickly."

Entering the clearing, they separated hands as Andrew got off the bike and they walked towards Erica's home. Even from a distance, it looked the same as when they'd first come here a few days ago, but he saw the modifications that Queen Nataganazar had clearly paid for—including what appeared to be a landing pad in the front yard. "I guess despite Victoria being on the outs with her mom, she wants her daughter to have the best."

Smiling, Erica said, "If you knew her personal wealth, this is less than a thousandth of a penny to the average person. In essence, this was nothing for her."

"Good to know for the future. I doubt she's out of the picture yet."

Much to Andrew's surprise, as they got closer to the house, another Centaur stepped out from around the side. It took him a tenth of a second to realize who it was, given how different she looked between now and when he'd last seen her. Gone was the blonde hair in the bun and the blue siding to cover her horse side. She had taken the liberty of applying makeup, tying up a shirt to expose her midriff as well as her breasts. Her hair flowed behind her like a wave of liquid gold reflecting off the sun. As before and with other women, he saw the heart-shaped locket hanging by a chain on her wrist.

Andrew was momentarily tongue-tied by her beauty, so Erica took the initiative. "Officer, what a pleasant surprise. How can we help you?"

"I am here for our—" Just one look from Tiffany's oldest friend made her correct her statement. "I just need to do some light follow-up with Erica in regards to the earlier problem with her mother, and I figured since I was in the area, I'd take care of it today."

"All right, let's talk outside." Turning to Andrew, Erica said, "Love, why don't you go inside and look up the ritual of Ratatitus? We'll be performing it tonight."

Once Andrew had left, Tiffany became more plain spoken, and, with a bit of an aggressive tone, said, "All right, Erica, what's going on? What's this ritual of Ratatitus? I did come here for our date night."

"No, you came here to be screwed, Tiffany."

Pulling back one side of her shirt, Tiffany showed that she didn't have a bra on. "If it happens, it happens, and it'd all be legal if you said the right words."

"For the record, the ritual of Ratatitus is when a gnome of either gender joins a new family, and, for whatever reason, wants their blood siblings to join that family as well. In this case, we have three sisters who are part-gnome, part-dwarf joining the family."

"And I take it this will be Andrew's first second wife? And how do the sisters fit into the clan?"

"Yes, and they'd be handmaidens. In essence, slaves of the clan. If they wanted anything, they'd be Bloom and Andrew's responsibility."

"Even sex?"

"Yes."

"Can I join in?"

Just by the tone of Tiffany's voice, Erica knew she wasn't serious. "No, but if you want to stay for it as a witness, you are free to." Blushing a bit, Erica looked down at her front hooves before saying, "And tonight, after the ritual is completed, I will tell Andrew who you are, and what your locket means."

"You promise?"

"On my honour as first wife, and lady of this clan."

Surprising Erica, Tiffany launched herself at her friend. Grabbing her, she brought Erica's face to hers and kissed her— not the kind of kiss one gives a child, but the kiss of a lover. Erica could feel Tiffany's tongue bury itself in her mouth. Just for a few moments, the Asian Centaur followed where her blonde counterpart led. She could feel herself becoming wet with arousal; now that she had a husband, she could let her friend go all the way. A dear friend who was reminding her why she'd agreed to offer her the position of one of her wives. Then it hit Erica like a freight train.

I. HAVE. A. HUSBAND.

Just like that, she stopped. Making out with her friend before she joined the clan was wrong. It was one thing to test Bloom, it was another to do it with Tiffany. Pushing Tiffany away, Erica said while panting, "We need to stop now!"

"We're just having fun like when we were fillies."

Stepping back a bit, Erica glared at Tiffany as she tried to compose herself. "We are not fillies anymore, Tiffany." Opening her eyes a bit larger to emphasize her point, she continued, "You lost the right to be first wife! I co-command this clan! While I can't offer you a date night with my husband tonight, you are free to go spend some time with him as I prepare for the ritual to welcome his first second wife into it." With that, Erica walked stomped off, making it clear to a dejected Tiffany how angry she was.

****

It had taken her some time, but Tiffany eventually worked up the mental resolve to enter Erica's home. She could not recall ever seeing Erica that angry, not for over twenty years of friendship. Over the years, she had been in this house countless times—usually to talk with Erica, hang out with her, sometimes to get an update on how the hunt was going for Mr. Right. For the first time she could remember, she felt like a stranger here.

It wasn't just the renovations that had been done to add several rooms to the home, it was the little things—like ramps for Charger to get up to the tops of tables. Where, even as a stranger to this home, the orange tabby cat ran up one and did everything he could to demand attention. Framed posters of movies she knew Erica had never seen waited along a wall for final placement.

With the shower running, she peaked around a corner and could hear Erica crying—something she never did. Then Tiffany heard something she thought was a myth; Andrew was consoling her. Not in the "grow up strong like your uncle" consoling, but like he...cared for her. Tiffany had always seen a husband as a sperm bank, a sex toy without batteries. Before, when Erica had told her about how Andrew cared for her, she thought it was a lie.

At least, that was how her father had been—making love to his various wives day or night, and not caring for them or the children. He was as uncaring as anyone could be—human, centaur, or lizardman. He'd come home, pick a wife, demand sex, and never seemed to care about them or his children.

Somehow, in the depths of her soul, she was shattered as she realized how wrong she was about Andrew by just listening to them. She had never even asked Erica why she was accepting the gnomes' ritual of Ratatitus. She had assumed it was so Andrew could have more women to fuck without even having to treat them as wives. Her friend had called herself co-leader of this clan, this family, and she was starting to realize how different it was from the one she'd come from.

Slowly backing out of the house, the only one who knew she had been there was Charger. She had some work to do, and amends to make. She wasn't going to be able to make them if she appeared to be stalking Andrew and Erica as they came out of the shower.

****

Andrew was looking himself and Erica over in the full-length mirror. He was dressed in a dark suit and tie, while Erica had put on a white robe with gold trim that covered her from her throat down to her hooves. Hanging around her neck was the heart-shaped locket she had been wearing when they'd got married. His face full of concern, Andrew asked, "Are you all right after what Tiffany did?"

"I will be, my love," she replied. "Thank you for asking for the tenth time." The playfulness could easily be heard in her voice.

"Just... It's been a wild ride for us. Three days ago, we barely knew each other, and now we're getting ready to welcome a gnome with her sisters into our clan. So, it's just us, the gnomes, and Victoria tonight?"

Straightening out his tie for him, Erica replied, "No, I invited my mother as well."

"What about Tiffany?"

"If she comes, she comes. I did invite her."

"As you wish."

Playfully smacking him, she said, "Smart man."

"I just worry about you. After your discussion with her, you seemed rather hurt."

Pulling his face towards her, she gave him a kiss. "And that is one of the many reasons I love you."

"So, besides showing up and reading off my tablet, is there anything special I need to do?"

Picking up two tablets off a nightstand, Erica passed one to Andrew. "No. In fact, the ritual of Ratatitus calls for the joining members to appear as poor as possible."

Andrew gave a laugh. "You know, a lot of my friends have complained about Bridezilla. This is my second wedding, and not one. I love it!" Following Erica out of their bedroom, he asked, "No need for some kind of holy book?"

Patting her tablet, Erica replied, "No. As much as we believe in honouring the past, we also modernize the rituals. Do you realize how many holy books we'd need if we used paper ones?"

"Twenty?"

Smiling, she shook her head. "More than you can imagine."

Entering the living room, one thing Andrew was becoming more accustomed to was that, in a sense, he felt small. As a larger man, he sometimes felt cramped in normal-sized places, but it seemed one of the benefits of marrying a Centaur was that there was plenty of space. Looking affectionately at Erica, it did make sense she'd want a home she felt comfortable in.

Across the room, he saw Erica's mother sitting in one corner, and opposite to her was Victoria. One appeared calm and collected, while the other seemed confused, which was normal for Victoria. Taking their spots in front of the TV, Andrew stood next to Erica.

Without having to look at her tablet, Erica said, "Friends and family, we are gathered here today to welcome not just a new wife into our clan, but her sisters as well." Like clockwork, the sound of gears turning filled the air. "A good family must be like a good machine, but sometimes a family falters, so we salvage what is good from it and improve another."

As if on cue, wearing nothing but rags that barely covered them and a gold bracelet on one arm, both Sherry and Hotwire entered the room. Crawling on their hands and knees, they approached Andrew and Erica.

Andrew hated that they had to do this, but he wasn't here to judge their rituals. At their feet now, Hotwire and Sherry said in unison, "Our family has fallen, please take us in! It was not our fault that it failed. The fault lies with the one that designed our family. He led us to poverty and defeat."

"While we respect your humility, you have nothing to offer us, go back to whence you came," Erica replied with a shooing motion, making it clear they were to leave.

"They might not have anything to offer your clan, but I do!" said Bloom as she walked into the room, the perfect image of confidence—her shortsword on her back, dark green leather armour that flattered her dwarven female figure, and her green hair in a tight bun. Getting down on one knee, and never breaking eye contact with Erica as she withdrew her blade and presented it to the Centaur, she said, "I offer myself as a second bride to your husband's side of the clan, and ask that you accept my sisters as handmaidens."

"While you are armed, what do you offer us? Do they know what it means to be handmaidens with a family?"

"I offer you knowledge and wisdom of the design flaws that led our old family to defeat. I offer my blade to protect you, and anyone else who joins this clan. If your husband were to accept me as his bride, then they would know only his touch unless they married out. They ask this out of desperation, but I wish to become one with your clan out of love. We ask your clan for mercy, so we may stay united. The one who led us to this is not among us."

Turning to Andrew, Erica said, "What say you, noble husband? Since, if these three are to have children, they will be the fruits of your loins. One of them does have spirit, and the other two do know humility." Both Sherry and Hotwire tried to act the role of being in dire straits. Given the minimal clothing they were wearing, it was easy to see bruises, cuts, and scars. He had seen enough injuries over the years to know the signs of abuse over a prolonged period of time. As far as Andrew was concerned, it all added up to what they had been told earlier.

While Andrew looked them over, Tiffany slipped into the unfolding drama holding a file folder. Wanting to confront her, Andrew made a mental note to talk with her once this was over. Holding out a hand, he said, "Noble wife, a ring, please, if you should agree with me."

Opening the locket, Erica pulled out a ring. "You understand what this means, noble husband?"

"I do."

Placing the ring in Andrew's awaiting hand, she said, "Then take this ring with the blessing of the first wife of this clan."

Getting down on one knee, Andrew looked all three gnomes in the eye. "Sherry and Hotwire, please raise your right hands."

They obeyed him. Focusing on Bloom, Andrew slowly picked up her sword, and then put it down with care. Then, picking up the gold ring, he said, "Bloom, your former clan has fallen, but I do love you. Will you accept this band as a token of my affection for you?"

"I do."

"Do your sisters understand the only way out of being a handmaiden is by marriage?"

"They do, my future Lord and Husband." Opening one of her hands, Andrew slid the ring on a finger.

"Then let it be known to all, that as of this day I accept thee as one of my second wives to love and to hold until the end of time."

Much to everyone's surprise, Erica said, "And let any who question our clan's decision to accept these women into our ranks know we did this for justice, honour, and mercy. Something our government would deny them due to laws not maturing with us as a people."

Andrew, Bloom, Sherry, and Hotwire rose up to face Mrs. Swifthood, Victoria, and Tiffany. Erica grabbed Sherry's hand, while Andrew grabbed Hotwire's, and both of them grabbed Bloom's to hold high. "I officially give you my husband's first second wife, along with our new handmaidens."

There was a smattering of applause. Looking down on his wedding ring, Andrew now saw on one side what appeared to be a green-haired gnome. It was official—if Jerry laid a hand on her, or her sisters now, he'd be violating the law. Despite what Bloom had said, he would have no problem defending his family as well.

Looking a bit sheepish, Tiffany approached the gnome sisters. "I know it's a human custom, but I have a gift for the bride and her sisters."

"Oh, I like gifts," said Bloom.

Passing her the folder, the Centaur said, "It contains the medical condition of Jerry, and includes express paperwork for you to secure ownership of Gnome Express."

"That's right, with us out of the family, we are given the right to kick Jerry out of the company!" said Hotwire.

"So we can kick him to curb like bad zombie parts!" said Sherry, who seemed close to laughing.

Picking up her sword and returning it to the scabbard on her back, Bloom looked up at Tiffany and said, "Why? We've been beaten before by him, why help us out now?"

Tiffany focused on Erica and Andrew. "Since sometimes we make mistakes, and we don't know how to say we're sorry any other way." Fingering the heart-shaped locket on her wrist, she said, "I hope one day my future husband will realize that we all make them when trying to understand the crazy directions that our lives take."

Erica looked from Andrew to Tiffany, and said, "All is forgiven, old friend. All we can do is learn and grow."

Flipping through the report, Hotwire commented, "I didn't know you could break one bone in so many places." Addressing everyone, she said, "Anyone mind if Sherry and I go change?"

"Yeah," Sherry agreed, fingering the rags she had been wearing. "These rags feel like something rejected from a nineteen-sixties caveman film."

"Go on, you two. Bloom, would you mind entertaining my mother and Victoria for a few moments while Andrew, Tiffany, and I speak outside privately?"

"Certainly."

Stepping outside, for reasons only Charger knew, he followed them. You could cut the tension hanging in the air with a dull butter knife given how thick it was. All three of them stood around on the grass. No one knew who should speak first until Tiffany did, addressing both Andrew and Erica. "I meant what I said in there—I am so sorry, Erica."

Erica couldn't keep the smile off her face as she replied, "This must be the first time in ages you've apologized for anything. What made it happen?"

Trying to keep the nervous look off her face, Tiffany said, "A lot of little things. I realized Andrew isn't my father, for one thing. I also did some research on Jerry. What he did was legal, but wrong. I understand why you did what you did today."

"Good to know. Now that that's in order, maybe we could have some formal introductions."

Erica pulled on both Tiffany and Andrew's hands to bring them both together, "Tiffany, could you hold up your arm with the locket, please?" Tiffany complied with Erica's request, holding her arm up so Andrew could see the locket easily. Erica continued, "Andrew, you've seen these before among our people?"

"Yes. I haven't had a chance to research them yet."

"It means Tiffany is someone's piewie, meaning 'promised wife.' It's like an engagement ring."

"All right, I am with you so far—Oh!" Both women saw his face light up. "Are you telling me what I think you're telling me?"

Giving a smile all men knew too well, Erica replied, "Yes, I am. Tiffany is one of my piewies; we've known each other since childhood. She helped me pay for my house in exchange for the right to join any family I create."

Andrew tried to keep cool and collected, but they could see his jaw drop a bit. "Does this mean you want her to join our family tonight?"

Both of them said, "No!" at the same time, causing them both to laugh.

Tiffany cleared things up. "When we met a few days ago, I blackmailed Erica into speeding up the process of when I could try to join your family. I was wrong, and totally out of line." Turning to Erica, she said, "When you feel it's time to tell Jessica you have a husband, it will be your choice. But if word gets out—and given what he is, it will—I am off the hook."

Erica just gave a simple nod of affirmation.

Tiffany shuffled her hooves a bit as she looked at Andrew. He had begun to realize it was a way Centaurs showed they were nervous. "I would still like to get to know you better, and then let you decide whether to veto me."

Nodding, Andrew said, "All right, Tiffany. All Erica told me earlier is that you had a fight and she was hurt. Just realize that if you hurt my wife again, all bets are off." There was something in his eyes that made Tiffany realize Andrew meant what he said with every ounce of his being, and she knew if he did accept her into the family, he'd do the same for her. "She might be your friend, but in this family, we watch out for each other."

Smiling, Erica took each of their hands. "With that in mind, I think we should go back inside and rejoin the party."

As Andrew led them back in, he didn't know it, but both female Centaurs took a moment to admire him from behind before escorting him side by side into the house. Tiffany hated to admit it to herself, but with his final statement to her, her opinion of Andrew had only gone up more.

As the party got into the swing of things, Andrew realized how many members of the human race would freak out about what was now becoming his life. Grabbing a drink from the fridge, he sat back on the couch and did something normal—he enjoyed life as he spent time with his new family.

****

Everyone had gone home for the night. Hotwire and Sherry had made alternative living arrangements, so they could honour the roles of handmaidens, but wouldn't be sleeping in the main house. While Victoria did have her own room, they had offered to dragon-sit for the night by sharing their quarters with her. Since, as far as the sisters were concerned, the wedding was just part of a much larger special day for Bloom, and they wanted to do everything they could to make sure it went perfectly.

Looking herself over in the bathroom mirror for what felt like the thousandth time, Bloom saw it all; the solid dark green silk baby doll lingerie set she had picked up really helped show off her body. The top ended just above where her panties started, and the top was cut to really show off her breasts. It had taken her a few hours to find one in a dwarf lingerie store that fit her with matching panties. Even then, the woman selling it to her recommended something with more leather in it.

However, she was one of nature, and unless it was for protection, it felt wrong to wear the skin of animals. Applying a final coat of green lipstick, she hoped she looked perfect. She was so confused—

part of her wanted Andrew to fuck her until she screamed, part of her just wanted to go to sleep. However, she knew it was normal to want to be with her husband like this on their wedding night. She heard Erica call out, "Bloom, you ready for bed yet?"

"J-J-Just a moment," she stammered out. Forcing herself to take a deep breath, in and out, she reminded herself who she was. She had beaten her abusive brother in more ways than one, she had a new family now. Yes, this would be the first time she shared her bed with a man, and he was a man who cared for her, and seemed next to impossible to faze.

Leaving the bathroom, she walked down the darkened hall towards the master bedroom. She spotted Charger sleeping on one of the bookshelves. She could feel her pussy burning with desire, her panties already soaked even though she had put them on not five minutes ago. Entering the bedroom, she paused at the door, totally surprised, her jaw dropped in shock. "Shouldn't you two be...?" she said to Andrew and Erica.

Both of them looked up from their tablets. Raising an amused eyebrow, Erica asked, "Shouldn't we be what?"

"I don't know, fucking like wild rabbits?" Bloom almost shouted from the door in shock. "Or engaging in other acts of hedonism?"

Getting up, the Centaur walked towards the gnome, as Andrew got out of bed himself, and sat down on the end of it.

Taking one of Bloom's hands, Erica walked her over to the end of the bed where Andrew made space for her in his lap. Bloom hadn't realized how normal they were dressed—Andrew was in an old t-shirt and black sweatpants, while Erica had on an old white t-shirt. They both appeared so relaxed, so casual about what was a big night for her. Andrew wrapped his arms around Bloom; there was nothing sexual about it, just a gentle, warm hug. Erica bent down so she could look the gnome in her eyes. "Bloom, there are two reasons why Andrew and I were not having sex when you came in."

Worry and doubt filled Bloom's eyes as she asked, "And they are?"

Looking to Andrew, he gave Erica a nod. "First, we wanted our complete family to be here when we had it."

"Okay, and the other reason?"

"We didn't want to feel we were pressuring you to have sex. If you just want to sleep, that's fine. We know this marriage isn't as much about sex as it is protecting you and your sisters from harm. Tonight we can all just go to bed and sleep." A familiar sugar-like smell began to fill the air, Andrew's hug became a bit tighter, and Bloom felt something poking her in the butt. Something that was growing by the moment.

"But if I wanted to make love tonight, neither of you would have a problem with that?"

Kissing her, the Centaur replied, "None at all, but tonight you are the center of the bedroom."

By expressing her desire to have sex, it was as if she'd unlocked them. Bloom felt one of Andrew's hands reach down to her panties, running a finger up and down them while his other hand began to massage her breasts. It only made her more eager for sex. "I think someone is a naughty gnome," he said playfully as he ran a finger along her vagina.

She had to focus to keep her eyes from rolling in the back of her head given the pleasure she was feeling. "I am naughty gnome, but only in the family."

One of Andrew's hands began to massage her clit directly, and he pulled her in for a kiss. She had waited so long for this moment. She heard Erica say, "Bloom, if you want protection, please let us know. We will not force you to have children against your will."

Andrew's tongue seemed to invade her mouth. Pushing him away for a moment, she blurted out, "No protection. Want children!" Before she knew it, he was back at it. She could feel a wetness developing behind her. *It must be pre-cum,* some part of her thought. As Andrew released her breast, she could feel Erica taking over, kneading them through the silk top she wore. It was becoming harder and harder to think, and she mentally giggled, given what was making it hard to think.

All this touching—it wasn't helping her, it was only making her feel like she was in a fire made of pure pleasure. Sweat was starting to spread all over her. She wanted relief, and, as if reading her mind, Erica got close to her and whispered, "You feel like you're on fire, don't you?"

"Uh-huh," Bloom murmured.

"Then maybe it's time you met the fire hose," the centaur said seductively.

As if perfectly timed, Andrew lay down on the bed, and Bloom turned around and got on top of him. He held her firmly to him, still kissing her. Sparing a glance downward, she saw a part of his erect penis sticking out from his sweatpants. Not asking, she pushed herself up so she could pull his shirt off. She admired the muscles in his shoulders. This is what she loved about human men—while she wasn't as tall as them, they were as wide as her.

"Show time!" she said as she reached for the bottom of the baby doll. She lifted it and flung it off. As she did so, she could feel her breasts move freely without constraint. It felt good to be topless; maybe it was something she could talk to Erica about, letting women in the family go topless if they wanted. Looking down at Andrew, who was now lightly playing with her breasts, she said, "Someone doesn't seem disappointed in the family goods."

Reaching up to her, he said, "Why would I?" as he started to kiss one breast, and work the other with one of his hands. In an instant, she was feeling more raw pleasure. *Dear lord,* she thought as he worked her over, *I have to get those hands insured.* It was like he knew on instinct which spots to touch without any guidance from her. She also knew what she really wanted, but couldn't ask because of how well he was handling her.

As if sensing the problem, Erica said, "Let me be of help. If you could push yourself up a bit, Bloom, please?"

Pushing herself up a bit, she saw Erica pull Andrew's sweatpants off of him. Now all that stood between Bloom and his cock were her panties. Given how things felt down there, she wondered if it wouldn't just find its way into her on its own, as if Andrew could somehow push her panties aside with his cock. "Now, Bloom, this is your last chance. If you say no, we will stop."

Grabbing Andrew by the hair, she brought his face up to hers, and could feel their teeth hit each other as they kissed. She wanted to be bumping uglies, as someone once put it, not teeth! With her hands wrapped around Andrew's head, she gave the Centaur a thumbs up.

She felt her panties being moved aside and heard Erica say, "Hold it in just a little longer, my loves."

Then it began. Penetration. One word did not do justice to the pleasure it was giving her. She could feel herself becoming one with Andrew. It was like when she'd first met him, and she'd made a rude play at him—something she knew she'd have to apologize for more formally soon. She was becoming one with him now in flesh to reflect how she felt in spirit.

It was going so slowly, she hated it, until she felt a spike of pain. She then heard Erica say, "Don't worry, that is normal." Something she did must've told the Centaur what she was experiencing.

Once the pain passed, it was a whole new kind of pleasure as Andrew's cock started to fill her up. It was like he somehow knew he had broken her, and was now doing everything possible to make amends. As he started to pound her—no, *dominate* her—with each thrust, she felt Erica slip her hand in so she could play with her clit, trying to kiss them both. She could feel the Centaur's breasts beside her own. They were really having sex as a family!

Just when she peaked and had to let go, she felt it. She felt Andrew fill her with his seed as they let loose cries of joy, and, for a reason she didn't know, he outlasted her as it seemed he dumped everything and more he had into her. Even as his cock shrank down to normal size, she could still feel his seed in her. It was like filling a hole one didn't know needed filling until it was done.

They released each other, and she collapsed beside him on the bed. She could hear him panting like her. When they had been together, she hadn't felt much sweat, but now that they'd slowed down, she did. "Thank you," she said between pants, adding, "Water, please?" She didn't even have the energy to open her eyes. Feeling a bottle of water being placed in her hand, she downed it. Throwing the expired bottle to the floor, she opened her eyes enough to see Erica's own purple ones looking down at her. Forcing herself up, she reached out and grabbed each of their hands, saying, "I mean it, thank you. Not just for this, but for everything. I will do my best to ensure this doesn't go unrewarded."

Smiling seductively, Erica replied, "Well, there is a way I think you could reward me."

"How?" Without even trying, Bloom could swear she was smelling sugar again.

"Ever heard the term 'lezzie show'?"

Shaking her head no, the Centaur explained, "It's what we did yesterday in the field, except Andrew watches us this time."

Then, to Bloom's surprise, he got up on his elbows and said, "Or I could join you two." Looking at him, Bloom's eyes expanded in surprise as she saw his cock getting larger again already. It was dripping with their mutual fluids.

"B-b-but humans—" she stammered out.

Smiling like an all-knowing woman, Erica interrupted her, saying, "Since we are legends and myths to most humans, is it not a surprise there are some myths about them among us?"

"True," Bloom confirmed as she adjusted to reality.

Adjusting himself, Andrew faced Bloom before kissing her, and one of his hands ran down to her nether regions, leading with a finger where moments before he had been slamming her with his cock and filling her with his seed. His thumb was already playing with her clit, and despite the pleasure it was giving her, she forced herself to speak as she pushed away from him. "Please stop, we need to talk for a moment."

Following her instructions, Andrew backed away, clearly confused and hurt. "Whatever you say, Bloom."

The sincerity in her eyes was obvious to everyone as she grabbed one of his hands and put it on her belly, just below her breasts. "I know second wives don't rank high when it comes to being given a child by the man of the family, but please know I do want one."

Looking to Erica, she said, "That means I am asking you don't eat me out, Erica, after Andrew..." She drifted off, unsure what to say next. One way sounded too crass, another sounded too light-hearted.

"I understand, Bloom, and I will respect your wishes," the Centaur said.

Getting up on the bed, Bloom walked up to Erica and planted a kiss square on her lips. "Beyond that, I am all yours." She sounded like someone in love. Looking at Erica, she said in shock, "And why are you still dressed?"

Erica seemed confused until she realized she still had an old t-shirt on. "Well, I—"

"Strip!" Bloom commanded. "Of all the nerve!" she said, stamping a foot on the bed. "Andrew and I are nearly naked and here you are still dressed." Everyone could tell she was kidding.

Getting up off the bed so he was eye level with his two wives, Andrew gave Bloom a gentle kiss on her cheek, "We respect your wishes, how about you respect Erica's?"

"All right," replied the gnome.

Looking at both Andrew and Bloom, there was something seductive in Erica's purple eyes as she removed the t-shirt she had been wearing. It was followed by a sigh of relief, as her breasts bounced free. "That old one is a bit on the tight side," she said, addressing them both.

Focusing on Bloom, there was something almost predatorial in Erica's eyes as she said, "As for you, my husband's second wife..." Forcing herself onto the gnome to kiss her, she pushed her, breast to breast, down onto the bed. "I will respect your wishes in regards to a child, but just remember who is first wife, and realize I might want one also."

Sounding almost breathless from the power of Erica's kiss, Bloom replied, "Naturally, my lady." With that, they resumed kissing before Andrew's very eyes. Andrew could see one of Erica's hands drift down to play with Bloom's clit. He watched in awe as the two large-breasted women made out. His cock had already semi-sprung to life, and now it was at full tilt. He no longer had to focus on when Erica became aroused— he could smell it in full force as it filled the air.

Getting behind the Centaur, he saw she had forgone any underwear, as was her nature. He casually ran a finger down her clit, feeling her buck from even his casual touch, despite her being focused on Bloom. Pushing her tail aside, he slammed his cock into her. He could feel her body greet him as it tried to hang onto his cock. With every thrust, he heard her moan with pleasure as she slowly released Bloom, until her own heavy breathing filled the air, and her cries of passion took over.

Andrew didn't know how long he held out, but he had learned how to hold back over the years. Still thrusting, he heard her scream louder and louder until it filled the room. Then they both came at the same time. He saw their combined fluids leaking out of her as his own legs threatened to give way. Staggering back towards the bed, he used Erica to help steady himself until he collapsed on it between Bloom and Erica, with his legs dangling off the end onto the floor. Erica's human half had likewise collapsed on the bed.

Rolling him over to face her, Erica gave him a passionate kiss. "Thank you. You mind if I half sleep on the bed tonight?"

"Not at all," he reassured her. It was something on the shopping list to find a bed Erica could share with Andrew and the other future wives.

Then Bloom rolled him over, and gently kissed him on the nose. "Thank you," she whispered to him. "You mind if we spoon tonight?"

"Not at all."

Bloom turned her back to him, promptly wrapping his arms around her, making sure his hands firmly grabbed her breasts. He could feel his cock growing erect a bit just by touching them, and she adjusted herself so she could it. "I think I could get used to this," Bloom said to no one in particular as she yawned and started to fall asleep.

Then, to Andrew's surprise, after throwing a blanket on them, he felt Erica start to snuggle up to him. "Goodnight, my husband. Pleasant dreams..."

With that, they all fell asleep.

Epilogue

In some ways, the last few days had taken a toll on Erica, Bloom, and Andrew, given how they all slept in past sunrise. No one from their respective jobs was going to risk waking them up.

Andrew was the first one to wake up, and found himself face to face with Bloom. Not wanting to wake anyone, he just lay there for a while, given how he could feel Erica still behind him. Then Bloom woke up. "Sleep well?" he asked her.

With a smile that would put the sun to shame, she whispered, "Best sleep I've had in decades." Moving to be closer to him, she whispered, "Sore in a good sense, and thank you."

Whispering back, he asked, "For what?"

Looking down, she said, "I know human courtship rituals take longer, and I wouldn't have asked for the ritual of Ratatitus if I didn't feel my sisters and I were in mortal peril." Looking him in the eyes, she continued, "Now if Jerry comes after us, he faces the law and our family." On saying the word "family," she launched herself at him in a hug, and he felt her entirely—from her breasts to her dried silk panties to her shaven legs that she wrapped around him. She was so overwrought with emotion that she was crying tears of joy. All Andrew could do was hug her back and console her. Holding back the tears, she said, "Thank you for taking a chance on me and my sisters. I know it won't always be easy, but thank you."

"I don't know what to say, Bloom, but I am willing to do everything I can to make this whole arrangement work." Bloom released Andrew a bit, allowing him to slide down off the bed. "And to that end, I think I'll go get some coffee and breakfast for my wives," he said, standing up to face her.

It was then that Erica chose to make it known to everyone she was awake by grabbing a pillow off the bed and playfully throwing it at Andrew as he left the bedroom, naked as the day he was born. "So it took a second wife to get you to treat me right?"

"Honey—" he started to say in his defence.

Cutting him off with a smile, she said, "No worries, my love. Just realize you have two wives here who are hungry in more than one way."

"But if we don't get food, we won't have the energy to fill the second hunger," Bloom contributed.

****

It didn't take long for Andrew to get three cups of coffee made; he didn't know what Bloom liked, so while he made some fresh muffins for Erica, he made some porridge for Bloom. As for him, he had his usual instant pancakes.

Navigating back to the bedroom with the trays containing the food was a bit harder than reaching the kitchen in the first place. While the construction crews had put up walls and added rooms, there was still a lot of work to be done. No doubt Queen Nataganazar had designs in mind she wanted to implement so her exiled daughter didn't have to live in what, as far as she was concerned, was a hovel.

Taking it all in, he realized that maybe this was their destiny—to be a family of exiles. Bloom had been exiled by her father due to misplaced loyalty in her brother. Andrew had never really fit in with the human race. Victoria, while not formally in the family, was on the outs with her mother. He wondered if Erica had been exiled in some way over the years. He had so much to learn about both women and these people if he was to be their ambassador to the human race.

Presenting the two trays—one to Erica, and one to Bloom—he rushed back to the kitchen for his own. Arriving in the bedroom, he put the tray on the bed as he grabbed his sweatpants to put on. Sitting down with his wives, he raised a coffee mug and said, "To family!"

Clinking their mugs with his, they replied, "To family."

We might be exiles, we might be misfits, but we will be able to become a family, he thought. *Wounds will heal, children will be born, and the future will be ours for the taking.* With that in mind, he hoped to enjoy breakfast in bed with his smiling wives.

Just then, the doorbell rang. Excusing himself, Andrew grabbed a blue bathrobe from the closet and made his way to the door.

Opening it up, he saw a short, balding, ginger-haired man waiting on the door step. He seemed quite wide, and was wearing a Hawaiian-style shirt and sunglasses. The man extended his hand and said something Andrew didn't understand.

Extending his own hand, Andrew greeted, "Good morning, how may I be of service?"

The unidentified man took Andrew's hand and shook it, and Andrew had to admit that, despite his smaller size, the other person had quite a grip. Speaking slowly, he said, "Good morning, I am here to summon Andrew to High Council, and to see my daughters."

"I am Andrew, and your daughters?"

Bloom had left the bedroom to see who was at the door, having thrown on a green bathrobe. At that moment, with her green hair askew due to bedhead, Andrew heard Bloom scream out in joy as she ran towards the door, "Daddy!"

"Daddy?" Andrew repeated before he collapsed.

****

While Andrew had collapsed for unknown reasons, Jerry was starting to recover from the beating Bloom had given him. That wasn't what the medical reports stated, though; according to the medical reports, he had suffered an accident while working. After all he had done for them, that weakling Bloom had the audacity to beat him up, he thought for the umpteenth time. In some cases, that was all he could do now—think. The list of his uninjured parts was far shorter than the list of body parts that were.

One of the nurses had been nice enough to set up a tablet nearby and he saw that he had received an e-mail that morning.

Jerry,

If you are reading this, it means you are awake. Guess you didn't suffer as badly in your accident as when we left to get help.

Sherry, Hotwire, and I have joined a new clan. This means you can't legally lay a finger on us without either facing the law or the wrath of our new clan. It also means that, given how Gnome Express is set up, we held a vote and you were fired. Arrangements will be made with the hospital for where to find your stuff and your fair share of the money for us taking over your twenty-five percent of the business.

While we wish you the best, Jerry, we want to make things clear. Come anywhere near us, and there will be consequences, as per the law.

Your Sisters,

Sherry, Hotwire, Bloom

If Jerry could have, he would have ripped up that letter and spat on it. He vowed then and there that this was far from over. Unlike humans who made family versus family violence illegal, among non-humans it wasn't. Once he recovered, he was going to crush his sisters and whatever family they had married into.

Those Dreaded Words From the Author

I want to thank you for taking a chance on me if you made it this far, since I admit this is my first completed book as an indie writer. For years, I did a load of fan fiction that I published on various sites, and I finally said it was time to try something new.

It's a daunting task looking at a blank page and asking yourself, "Where do I go from here?" At least with fan fiction, you have rules. Here, there are none except those you make yourself.

I also want to thank my friends, family, and people I play various online games with for putting up with me as I bounce ideas off of them. Writing is a solitary kind of thing—you need the social contact to help keep you sane.

Just to be clear, the name James Lyon is a pen name, and, trust me, it's a well-known right of authors. Mark Twain became better known by that name than his real one. I did my best to avoid any real-world names or products due that evil thing called lawyers. I mean, come on, would you want your multi-billion dollar brand to be mentioned in a two-bit erotica novel? Maybe in the next one we'll see brands we recognize.

Now I know I was evil leaving things on a cliffhanger. There is a sequel that, as of this book's publication, is called *Broken Souls*. As of writing, *Broken Souls* is at least two to three months away from being published. Realize, it takes me about a year to a year-and-a-half to write and edit each novel. I am hoping to cut down the production time, but no promises.

This is something I do on the side, and while I do hope it might become a viable carrier, I've also got to do normal jobs to pay the normal bills.

Just to answer some questions I expect to get... I used Word

2007 to write this book. Yes, I paid someone for that excellent piece of art that is the cover. The guy had no reference photos, but he did a smashing job, if I do say so myself.

What happens next?

Well, you can reach out to me at James__Lyon@hotmail.com, or wait for it...

Join the Author James Lyon Fan Group on Facebook where I will post weekly (or try to) updates on my upcoming novels.

www.ingramcontent.com/pod-product-compliance
Lightning Source LLC
Chambersburg PA
CBHW070040260626
47159CB00005B/2088